THE 7000 SOULS OF ALMA DRAKE

MARIE FLANIGAN

For my husband, Colin, all the love.

The 7,000 Souls of Alma Drake
Red Adept Publishing, LLC
104 Bugenfield Court
Garner, NC 27529
https://RedAdeptPublishing.com/

---

1.   http://StreetlightGraphics.com

Chapter 1: Bowling Ball Head

I'm a monster. I know that. Some people might think I'm a whore, but I'm not, although some men do end up paying for the privilege of dying. A girl's gotta eat. Other than the monster part, I'm like most people: I've got a job to do, debts to pay. I need food, shelter, and clothing. That and to quench my insatiable thirst for the souls of men.

Which is why I'm here, at the Vienna Inn, on a Tuesday morning at seven a.m. It's a little early for most of the sex trade, but this place is going to be hopping with deputy sheriffs coming off the midnight shift in about five minutes. You might think tapping an officer of the law is risky, and if I were a regular criminal, that might be true. Lucky for me, sucking out a man's soul looks exactly like a heart attack when a doctor is doing the autopsy. Well, unless it's a witch doctor. Witch doctors can tell the difference right away. And in some countries, I could be torn apart on sight by a group of savvy villagers. Fortunately, I live in the good ol' US of A. Here, people walk right by me without even noticing. It's kind of horrible.

Ah, but enough of that. Here come the sheriffs or, as other succubi and incubi call them, prey. Today's offerings are pretty good. Two women—we can ignore them. A big black guy—he's hot but entirely too fit and healthy for my needs. I say doctors can't tell, but there's no point in pushing it. Let's see, a tough little Hispanic guy—he's out. Oh! Here he comes, a great big white guy, all red-faced with his gut falling over his belt and probably on the verge of a heart attack anyway. He's perfect. My target has a big round head with his hair cropped in a high and tight. I shall call him Bowling Ball Head, BBH for short.

I set my face and sidle up to him. He's literally bellied up to the bar, and his mind is obviously on drinking because he doesn't notice me at first, which is irritating because this is my good face, my hot face, my come-fuck-me face. Oh, wait. That's the problem. It's early. I'm not quite awake. I retool my features to be more vulnerable, less hot. Because, realistically, this guy isn't going to talk to hot women. History tells him he doesn't get hot chicks. I morph my figure into something less magazine-perfect and more like a regular woman who's lived hard. I darken circles under my eyes and lean into the bar the way he does. He notices. Score.

"Hey," he says as the bartender slides him a beer.

I nod at him.

"You just gettin' off shift?"

I nod again. "Yeah, long night."

"Me too," he says and takes a sip of his beer.

"You a cop?" I ask. Men love it when they can correct you.

"I'm a deputy. I work over at the jail."

"Oh. That sounds rough."

He puffs his chest out a bit. "It can be. Nothing I can't handle."

I look him over. "I bet there's not a lot you can't handle."

He actually blushes a bit. "Oh, well." He takes a sip of beer.

Oh, good grief. How long are we going to have to play this game? I would never have picked him if I'd thought he'd be hard to get. He's still the best target in the place, though, and I'm hungry, so I don't want to go anywhere else. I fish a pack of cigarettes out of my bag, along with a lighter I know doesn't work.

I try to light my cigarette. He doesn't immediately offer me a light. No wonder this guy's got no ring.

I touch his hand. "Hey, do you have a light?"

Touching his skin is important. Now, even if I can't get him in his car out back, I won't lose track of him. Losing track of him would be bad, very bad. This way, I can scent track him anywhere.

A waitress glares at me. "You can't smoke that in here."

"Oh, right," I say, feigning dejection. "Sorry."

I start to put away the cigarette. I don't really smoke, but it's often convenient for pulling in prey. Smokers are chatty with one another because their addiction is a lot less socially acceptable than it used to be. They bond over how inconvenient that is.

He pulls a lighter out of his pants pocket and looks at my hand, which is still on his. I can see the disbelief cross his face. He can't believe his luck, doesn't believe his luck, but goes for it anyway.

"You wanna smoke it outside?"

Bingo. "Yeah, I sure do."

I follow him out to the parking lot. He walks me over to a late-model black F-250 with a double cab, tinted windows, and jacked-up wheels parked in the corner of the tiny lot. He leans against it. I could kiss him, so I do. Grabbing his belt, I lay one on him. His mouth tastes like beer, and I can smell a night's worth of sweat and jail stench on him. It doesn't matter. Stuff like that used to bother me, but now it's just part of the job. I'm sure you don't like every little aspect of your job either.

BBH is feeling his groove. He stuffs the lighter back in his pocket and fishes out his keys. He's got one hand on my ass while he's aiming his keys with the other. I can feel him already getting hard. This'll be a piece of cake. I'll definitely have time for a latte after. I hear the doors unlock.

We crawl into the back, and he reaches for me. "Come to Papa," he says.

"Oh, no," I say, pressing my hand against his chest and pushing him back. "You sit back. Let Mama do all the work."

"All right," he says, undoing his belt.

Now, here's the thing. He's expecting a blow job. I'm not interested in blow jobs. They don't get me anything. Oh, sure, I know the medieval texts about succubi say we're after sperm, but we're not. I couldn't care less about sperm. It does nothing for me. What I want is this poor bastard's soul. And the deal is souls are slippery. They can get away from you. Can I suck this guy's soul out of his dick? Absolutely, but if he opens his mouth while I'm doing it, his soul can slip out, and catching a disembodied soul is a huge pain. No soul wants to be captured by a demon, and I'm a demon, so I cover my bases.

I drop my pants and underwear and saddle up. That might sound quick, but I don't need foreplay. It just slows me down. Besides, I assure you, BBH isn't worrying about that right now. I grab his face, pull his mouth to mine, and suck like my life depends on it—because it does. Less than a minute later, BBH is wide-eyed and gasping for his last breath. I sit with him and hold his hand. No one should have to die alone. When he exhales his last, I go through his wallet and take the cash. He has twenty-seven dollars and fifty-three cents on him. Breakfast.

"Sorry, buddy," I say to BBH's slumped form. I tuck him back in and zip him up. There's no reason for him to be a seedy headline on the news at noon. He was a nice-enough guy.

I look around before I slip out of the truck. It's not like it really matters if anyone sees me, but just to be safe, I check. All clear.

As I walk away from the parking lot, I shift my face and my figure. If anyone had seen me in the bar, they'd never be able to identify me now. I feel good. I've got five warm souls jiggling around inside me. It's satisfying and makes me feel almost whole. I'm drunk on it and happily cutting through parking lots on my way to the café one street over, which is probably why I don't notice that bastard Ian.

He grabs my arm and yanks me into a narrow alley between office buildings. Instinctively, I show my true face. It's not pretty, but Ian is unfazed by my razor-sharp teeth and glowing yellow eyes. He flashes his own true face, which is scarier than mine, the incubus prick.

"You have something that belongs to me."

He licks the side of my face, and as much as I would like to shove his head through the brick wall behind him, I stand there and take it. I know for a fact he can beat me in a fight. Besides, I do owe him. All five of my hard-earned souls are his for the taking. Bastard.

Faster than you can imagine, he shoves his hand into my mouth. He sticks his whole arm down my throat. (It's as awful as it sounds.) When he pulls back his hand, he sticks it in his mouth and sighs with contentment. While he's all fat and happy, my full, happy feeling is gone. Now I'm ravenous and empty. I snarl at Ian, but he only laughs before slapping me hard across the face.

"Stop hoarding souls," he growls, and I can feel the hot stench of his breath on my face. "Don't make me track you again."

I pull away from him, but he just laughs at me as he saunters out of the alleyway. I hate him. It's his fault I'm in this mess in the first place. I read once that an incubus had sex with a woman to impregnate her with his demon seed. Ridiculous. They suck out souls, just like I do, but some incubi—strong ones, old ones—can hold a soul for ransom. Ian has my soul. And for the low, low price of seven thousand souls, I can have it back. Bastard.

So much for breakfast. I'm hurting now, and sex at this hour is almost impossible. All the sheriffs have finished their breakfast and gone home, along with all the other late-shift workers, and normal people are at work. It's almost impossible to pick up anyone from about eight o'clock in the morning until around six p.m. People may have trysts at lunch but not generally with strangers. I'm sure some people do, but I don't have time to hunt for a needle in a haystack. I'm hurting, so I do what anyone would do. I go home. I can scroll through hookup apps from bed.

It takes me a while to find my car. Yes, I drive. Most demons do these days. I don't know any of those mystical flying types you read about in stories. I'm guessing the demons in New York City probably take public transportation like everyone else. But I live just outside DC, and around here, we mostly drive. I fumble with the keys when I get to my car. I feel like there are razors in my gut. Fucking Ian, he didn't have to take all five souls. He could have left me one, something to hold on to, just one soul to push back the pain. It's not like he needed all five. He must have twenty succubi working for him. He eats a ton of souls. Greedy bastard.

It's hard to drive doubled over, but I go slow and do my best. Traffic is heavy, so it's not like anyone else is going over twenty-five miles an hour either. It takes me forty-five minutes to do a twenty-minute drive. By the time I pull into the driveway, I'm sweating. My mom must have heard me pull in, because when I fall out of the driver's-side door, she's there to help me up. Yeah, you heard me. My mom. I wasn't always a monster, and even if I had been, everyone's got a mother.

"Oh, Alma," my mother clucks as she helps me into the house.

My mother is under the impression that I'm a junkie. To help this impression along, I make red tracks appear on my arms.

Mom helps me into bed and goes to make me something to eat. You'd think she'd be pushing me into rehab, but luckily, she was codependent on my drugged-up father for so long that she just *tsks* at me and makes a sad face. Trust me when I say she's fine with having a junkie for a daughter, but a soul-sucking demon would scare the crap out of her. Hell, it scares me.

A big bowl of chicken soup helps some with the pain. Laugh if you want, but chicken soup's magical powers are totally real. Demons swear by chicken soup, just like humans. It cures what ails you but not forever. All I can do now is sleep until evening and scroll through the apps, and then I've got to go out again. I can go maybe twenty-four hours without a soul, and then I start to lose my ability to disguise who I am. Seventy-two hours without a soul, and I'm dead. And I don't mean undead. I mean really dead, nothing-but-dust dead. I'm trying to avoid that.

Chapter 2: The Jerk

When I wake up, it's late. Mom's already gone to bed. I microwave myself another bowl of miracle soup and then get dressed. I'm going to the Ritz tonight, so I have to be dressed to the nines. Luckily, all that requires is one really expensive little black dress and my own personal brand of charm. If I'm lucky, I might bag two souls tonight. Two would be good. Two would be very good. The Ritz Carlton in Alexandria is a haven for wealthy travelers—lonely, wealthy travelers. My favorite. I check my look in the mirror. I look amazing. When I put it on, I really put it on.

The bar is crowded when I arrive. Convenient. I like choices. It's all muted tones and modern lighting in here. The tablecloths are crisp and white. The flowers are real and fresh. The candles on the tables cast the whole place in a glow of warmth and money, but desperation rolls off this crowd like sweat. They're desperate to achieve, desperate to be better than the next guy, desperate to show they've still got it, desperate for a drink, desperate to get laid. That last part is a winner for me.

I grab a scotch at the bar and start to sniff around the room. I mean literally sniff around the room. Since I became a demon, my sense of smell is incredible. I feel like I know how a hound experiences the world now. It's weird but useful. There's a mature gentleman in the corner who smells like advanced cancer. I'm just about to shift into something a little older when the Jerk walks in. I'm sure you've met this guy. He's wearing a three-thousand-dollar suit and sporting a hundred-dollar haircut. His nails are manicured. Unexpectedly, he sits next to the mature gentleman.

"So, Oscar," the Jerk starts. "Rough day?"

"It was fine," Oscar says.

Clearly, Oscar wishes the guy would leave him alone, but apparently, the Jerk delights in pestering Oscar.

"You thought those sales numbers were fine?"

The Jerk grips Oscar's shoulder. Oscar winces.

"No wonder your star is fading, man. Let me buy you a drink."

The Jerk has a big grin on his face. I hate him. Oscar hates him. I'm starting to like Oscar, so I think I'll do him a favor.

"I already have a drink," Oscar says.

The Jerk claps him on the back. "I'll get you another. You need it after a day like today."

When the Jerk steps over to the bar, I shoot a stream of pheromones his way that would cripple a horse. This costs me. I'm soulless right now. I should conserve energy, but I don't want this one to get away. Like flies to honey, he comes right to me.

"Hey," he says, stepping into my personal space. He smells like expensive men's cologne, not too much, just the right amount. "You are the most beautiful creature I've ever seen."

I smile my most inviting smile. "Creature" is right.

"What are you drinking?" he asks.

This guy looks like a single-malt-scotch snob. I lie and say "The Balvenie" because it's the only expensive scotch I can think of. I'm actually drinking Johnnie Walker Red.

He smiles. "Ah, nice. Have you tried the Ardbeg Uigeadail?"

"Not yet."

His smile broadens. "Then let me enlighten you."

"Please."

Good grief. I wish I could suck out his soul right here and be done with it. As he orders my drink, I'm already beginning to regret this plan. This is what I get for impulsively picking a target because I don't like him instead of sticking to the tried-and-true sap. I finish my scotch.

Sure, the alcohol is helping with the pain in my gut, but my ravenous cravings are so bad my ears are roaring, and now this guy wants to impress me. Crap. On the exceedingly small chance this guy doesn't invite me up to his room, I graze his fingers with mine as he hands me the drink.

The Ardbeg Uigeadail is incredibly smooth. Good night, Johnnie.

"So, what do you do?" the Jerk asks.

"Mostly, I dabble in other people's projects. What do you do?"

This is the perfect answer, because despite the Jerk's question, he doesn't care what I do. He won't ask what I meant by dabbling. Instead, he will immediately launch into his favorite subject, himself.

"I'm in surgical sales. My company provides the industry's top implements to the world's top doctors. And as of today, I'm salesman of the year. Again."

I smile at him like I care about his success. "We should celebrate."

His smile broadens into a grin. "Yes, we should. Would you like to celebrate here or someplace more private, like my room?"

I slide a finger under his tie and stroke it. "Private sounds nice."

"Then private it is."

He leans across the bar and asks the bartender to have a bottle of Dom Pérignon sent to his room then takes my hand and helps me off the barstool. He salutes poor Oscar as we walk by. Jerk.

His room is exactly like I expect it to be. He takes off his jacket and hangs it in the closet. All of his personal items are precisely laid out. This guy is meticulous. The room has a king-size bed.

He smiles at me. "What do you think?"

I decide to take a dig at him through his wallet. "The Ritz always has such lovely rooms. Were no suites available?" Score. I see it cross his face as clearly as if I'd struck him.

"No," he sputters. "My company made the reservation, and they're a bunch of tightwads."

"Oh well," I say, running my hand down his tie again. "We'll make do."

That perks him back up. There's a knock at the door. While he goes to get the champagne, I step over to the window. His room has a nice view of Alexandria, although you can't see the river. I watch the ebb and flow of traffic on the street below until he stands behind me, pressing his chest to my back. Wrapping his hands around my waist, he kisses my neck.

As with every other aspect of his life, the Jerk is meticulous about making out. There's no passion, but there is a great deal of precision, as though he's memorized a manual and is going through each step. When I let out a soft sigh at his kiss, he moves his hands up to cup my breasts. I consider briefly letting him do his thing, letting him impress me with all his slick moves, but I'm hungry, and he's boring. I turn around in his arms, and he kisses me. He's a good kisser, not too wet, not too dry. He doesn't try to devour my lips. Then he steps back from me and smirks. He knows he's a good kisser.

I purr at him and lean in and whisper in his ear. "You're good."

"Baby, I'm just getting started."

Stroking my hand over his crotch, I squeeze just a little. "You know what I'd like?"

"Tell me, baby. I'll give it to you any way you want it."

"I'd like it right here up against the window. I want the whole city to see us." This hits all his buttons. He's rock hard.

"I like the way you're thinking," he says, unzipping his fly.

I drop my thong, and he hoists me up, giving me room to wrap my legs around him. He's inside me in one stroke. I smile at him. I can see the strain of holding me in the cords of his neck, but he's in it to win it. Just to be mean, I flash my real face. He's horrorstruck as I grab his head and latch on to his lips. I suck for all I'm worth, but it's a singularly unsatisfying experience.

As his body starts to fall backward, I can't get off of him fast enough and fall to the floor with him. Disentangling myself, I kick at him with my foot. What a waste of time—this guy's soul is so malnourished that it's barely a snack. Growling, I retrieve my underwear. Stupid jerk. On the other hand, his wallet yields four hundred thirty-two dollars. At last, some serious walking-around money.

The elevator ride gives me an opportunity to assess my options. I briefly consider going back to the bar at the Ritz, but those guys are too much work. My best bet is probably one of the truck stops on Route 1. Luckily, I keep a too-tight, too-short V-neck top and a tight pair of jeans in my trunk.

Even though the garage at the Ritz is well lit, I get a creepy feeling on the way to my car, like someone is watching me. Surely, Ian couldn't be after me again so soon. I haven't had enough time to hunt. I look around. Maybe I'll luck out and a mugger or a rapist will jump me. That would be so convenient—like delivery! Alas, it's a low-crime area. I don't see anyone, and no one conveniently offers up his soul for my consumption. Meanwhile, the Jerk's tiny little soul is flopping around in my belly doing next to nothing. I've never eaten such a small soul. What the hell was wrong with that guy?

Chapter 3: The Old Biker

The truck stop doesn't have many truckers. Believe it or not, there are two driving couples and half a dozen guys, none of whom gives me a second glance. I alter my appearance slightly and take a seat at the counter. Everyone else is in booths, and none of them are solo. They're all chatting like long-lost friends, and it feels more like a sewing bee than a truck stop. What's wrong with these guys? Who doesn't want a quick hookup? Apparently, these people.

Frustrated, I head to a biker bar down the road. Back before I became a demon, I never went to biker dives or truck stops—or fancy bars at the Ritz, for that matter. I wasn't big into partying or drinking or casual sex. I used to wonder why Ian chose me when this clearly wasn't my scene, but knowing him as I do now, I know why. He thought it was funny: let's turn a shy, quiet girl into a succubus and see what happens. What a joke! Yeah, it's a real laugh riot, let me tell you.

As fate would have it, there is one gray-haired biker still willing to show a lady a good time. He has a deep voice and kind eyes, and he reminds me of Sam Elliott with long hair. I age myself up a bit because he doesn't seem the type to want too young of a woman. I shoot for what I think looks twenty years younger than him. I'm figuring him for around sixty, but some of these guys live really hard, so he could be forty for all I know.

He tells me his life story. I actually listen, because even though I'm hungry, he's lived an interesting life. He grew up in Portland, worked crab boats in Alaska, then drove big rigs in the lower forty-eight. In his late thirties, he went to school to work on big trucks. He owned his own shop for a while but overreached in the nineties and lost it in the crash. He's working part-time for a shop down the road but hoping to go full-time soon. He asks about me, and I tell him a version of the truth: kind mother, druggy father, college dropout, currently unemployed. He actually encourages me to go back to school. What a sweetie. He asks me if I want his zip hoodie as we step into the chilly night air. I tell him I'm still warm from the beer. He holds my hand as we walk back to the cheap motel where he's living. His hands are big and callused.

At the shabby but tidy motel room, the old biker offers me another beer. Instead of accepting, I kiss him. He is nice, unhurried, and gentle, so after I suck out his soul, I comb his steel-gray hair and braid it down his back before laying him out on the bed. I pull the blanket over him, and he looks like he could be sleeping. I hate my life.

He only has a dollar and seventy-one cents in his wallet, so I leave it there. I also make it clear he'd been with a woman before he died. I leave my thong on the floor and give him a couple of lipstick-heavy kisses. I figure the old guy would've liked to go out like Attila the Hun, and now he'll be a legend in this place. (In case you're worried about the police thinking this is a suspicious death and testing the thong for DNA, don't. Demons don't leave DNA. Silver lining.)

Unlike the Jerk, the biker's big, warm soul leaves me feeling much better, but as I slip out of his motel room, I again get that sensation of someone watching me. It can't be Ian, because that greedy bastard would have jumped to grab my fresh soul right away. As a demon, you learn to trust your feelings and intuition in whole new ways. Someone is watching me, and it bothers me that I can't see or even smell them. I might actually have to go to Ian with this. He's a bastard, but he knows more than I do, and in a pinch, he'll protect his investment—namely, me.

Chapter 4: Ian

I can hear my mother stirring in her bedroom when I get home. I quickly sneak a couple of twenties into her purse. I try to help out with household expenses when I can, but if I put in too much at a time, she notices and wants to know how I got the money. As you can imagine, that's an impossible conversation. I don't want her thinking I'm turning tricks for cash. I guess I sort of am, but she doesn't need to know that. I've tried to get a regular job a couple of times, but between hunting all night and dealing with Ian, it's impossible to keep one, so I put a few bucks in my mother's purse when I can. So much for daughter of the year.

Mom comes out and makes me breakfast. Eggs and toast aren't chicken soup, but they're better than nothing. I kiss her cheek before heading off to my room.

I lie in bed, contemplating my situation. Seven and multiples of seven are magical numbers in the world. Seven souls is a magical number for succubi. If I could manage to consume seven souls, I would feel whole, almost like I had my own soul back. Sadly, I've never had more than five at a time. I don't know how he does it, but Ian has a sixth sense about these things. Technically, I'm supposed to go to him every time I accumulate three—to give him two and keep one to sustain me while I hunt for more. But finding him is a hassle, and the more souls I have, the better I feel. So maybe I'm not big on following the rules. As you've seen, Ian is.

So before I look for him, I find a meth addict who can still get it up and take his soul, so I have something to offer Ian. Atypically, Ian manages to be in the first place I look.

I don't know how old Ian is, because demons don't age like humans do, but I figure him to be pretty old. He has a townhome in Georgetown, and if I'm not mistaken, it belongs to him. These days, in the era of computers and enlightened security, it would be difficult to pull off something like that unless you could pay cash or work with some older demon to make it happen. That's difficult, because demons have a tendency to hate each other. The vast majority of us much prefer human company to that of other demons. Perhaps that's why we don't run the world. Right now, I don't have time to explore that philosophically, because miracle of miracles, Ian's home. I can smell him.

I knock on the ornate door of the three-story brick home.

He enjoys making me wait, and I stand outside for several minutes. After a while, his big yellow eye appears in the peephole, and I fight the urge to poke it. Then the door opens, and I step into one large room. He's removed the floors between the stories and all the interior walls. A steel frame now supports the structure, in the middle of which stands Ian, in all his red-skinned demon-ness.

His place stinks to high heaven. I wonder how his neighbors can stand it. The place is a mess because Ian never throws anything away. Clothes, books, and empty food cartons are everywhere, and for some reason, the entire ceiling is black, as if a massive fire had occurred. Weird but not weird enough for me to ask.

Ian growls at me. "This is unexpected."

"I brought you a prize," I say and reach down my own throat and pull out the meth addict's soul and the Jerk's pitiful soul.

Ian smiles and pulls my fist into his mouth and sucks them out of my hand. He licks his lips. "One of those was pretty paltry."

"Asshole sales guy."

Ian sucks his teeth. "Okay, so what do you want?"

"You told me not to hoard souls, so I brought you some."

He narrows his eyes at me. "I've told you not to hoard since I made you, and you always do it anyway. Why the sudden change of heart?"

The smell in here is making me gag. I wish we could go outside, but Ian is in his true form and definitely not in the mood to go out.

"Someone's watching me."

He runs a long black claw over his lips and taps the sharp point of it against his teeth. "Who?"

"I don't know. I can't see him or smell him, but I know he's there."

Ian frowns, and the red tint of his skin darkens. He doesn't say anything. He just keeps tapping his claw against his teeth.

"You think I'm crazy."

"On the contrary. You're the third person to tell me someone is watching them this week."

That surprises me. "Really? Someone's watching other succubi?"

"One was a succubus. The other was a poltergeist."

"How do you watch a poltergeist? I thought they were invisible."

"Yes. That's rather the point."

When he's in his true form, his elocution improves. It's disturbing for something so scary-looking to speak so eloquently.

"You have friends who are poltergeists?"

"Don't be ridiculous," he says with a grimace.

"What? You were the one talking to him." Demons are so sensitive.

"I only met him because he haunts this row of houses. Out of a sense of professional courtesy, I told him to stay out of my way or I would eat him."

"And he told you someone was watching him?"

"Yes. I ran into him last week, and he mentioned he might look for a new area because he had the sense someone was watching him here. He asked if I had any suggestions."

Hmm. Something didn't seem right to me. "Wait a minute. Isn't a poltergeist a ghost?"

Ian nods and starts tapping his teeth again. It's a very annoying sound.

"We can eat ghosts?"

"Of course," Ian says, as if it were the most obvious thing in the world. "Ghosts are souls. Disembodied, yes, but still souls. Of course, just because we can eat them doesn't make it easy. It's quite difficult, actually. I doubt you'd be able to manage it."

"Huh. I didn't know that."

"You're a baby. You don't know a lot of things. You're practically still human."

"I will be again too." I cling to my humanity in every way I can. For instance, unlike Ian, I don't sit around in my true form. It's creepy.

"You say that now." Ian sighs nostalgically. "But there are advantages to being a demon you can't see yet. One day, when you're stronger and you've spawned some demons of your own, you'll see things differently."

Something about him suddenly reminds me of my mother and sends a chill down my spine. I need to shift the subject back to the matter at hand. "Right, so about this thing that's watching us—"

"Ah, yes. I'll look into it. In the meantime, try not to be too conspicuous."

"I suck out men's souls and leave a trail of dead bodies behind me. I can only be so inconspicuous about that without starving to death."

He gives me a big grin and pinches my cheek. "Which is why, Cupcake, it's so nice to have others come and feed you."

Bastard!

Chapter 5: Two for One

Leaving Ian's apartment, I gulp in fresh air. It's nice to just stand in the sunshine for a minute and enjoy the quiet street where Ian lives, but almost immediately, the hair on the back of my neck stands up. Someone's watching me again. I hurry down the block to where my car is parked. Instinctively, I glance at the window to make sure I haven't gotten a parking ticket. It takes a PhD in linguistics to understand the street parking signs in DC, but I never even finished my bachelor's degree, thanks to Ian. I usually just park where I see other cars and hope for the best. I'm lucky today—no ticket. I'm ravenous now that I'm down to one soul, but it's midday and pickings are slim, so I decide to go home.

Mom is still in her bathrobe when I arrive. She's opening cabinets and muttering to herself.

"Hey," I say as I walk in the door. "What's up?"

"I can't find my glasses," she says and continues to walk through the house, looking.

I open the fridge to get something to drink and some of yesterday's chicken soup to reheat. My mother's glasses are on the top shelf of the fridge. "Mom?"

She appears at the kitchen door. "Yes?"

I hand her the glasses. "They were in the fridge."

She looks at them as if they're unfamiliar for a moment. "I don't know why they'd be in there."

I shrug. "You've got a lot on your mind, that's all. You probably set them down when you were getting something else. Can you heat up this soup for me?"

Sticking her glasses in her pocket, she takes the container of soup. I could heat it up myself, but somehow, it tastes better when she does it. The soup does the trick, and Mom goes to change for work. I have a wave of guilt about her working and taking care of me. I promise myself I'll be a better daughter before heading up to take a shower and go to bed.

It's late afternoon when I wake up. There is a white claw on the pillow next to me. I leap up, frightened out of my mind, and the white claw leaps with me. Yeah, that's because it's mine. Somehow, I'd shifted to my succubus form in my sleep. What the hell? That hasn't ever happened before. Was I just really tired, or is my humanity slipping away? That's too scary to contemplate. I slip into my old form and head downstairs to vacuum and dust the living room as a surprise for my mother. Do evil, soul-sucking demons who've lost their sense of humanity vacuum for their mothers? I don't think so. I'm fine.

I microwave more chicken soup before I head out for the night. As I stand waiting for it to heat up, I contemplate my options. I'm pretty hungry. The soup will help, but I really can't fool around tonight: Mama needs souls. Despite yesterday's failure, I decide to revisit the truckstop plan. Tonight's outfit: tight jeans, a tank top that's a couple sizes too small, and no bra. I slip on a pair of sandals, and I'm good to go.

Route 1 was a bust yesterday, so I think I'll head up 95 into Maryland. I've been killing too many people close to home lately, and Ian's warned me against doing that. Besides, who would expect to find me so far north? Maybe I can throw off whoever's been following me. It's odd, though, because I don't ever get the sensation of being watched when I'm at home. Why would someone suddenly stop watching me because I went home—wouldn't that be the easiest place to watch me? It's a sigh-worthy quandary.

The truck stop is pretty empty when I pull in. There are two big rigs parked next to each other and only two other cars. I take a space in the back as far from the door as I can. I check my look in the reflection from the car window before I go in. The clothes are right, but my hair is wrong. I make it bottle blond with dark roots and add a touch of too-red lipstick, and my look is complete.

When I walk into the truck stop, there are two guys laughing in a booth and a lone waitress working behind the counter. She looks like she's had better days. Behind her, a cook in a stained white T-shirt works the grill. I take a seat at the counter and check out the menu. They have chicken soup. Score.

"Hey," the waitress says. "What can I get you?"

"Can I just get a bowl of chicken soup and a Coke?"

"Sure."

She sets the soup in front of me, and one of the guys from the table yells, "Hey, baby, can we get some more coffee over here and some of that apple pie?"

He has bright-yellow hair, and it irritates me the way he calls the waitress "baby." I'm going to reserve judgment for the moment, because maybe he's the waitress's boyfriend. But I shall call him Piss Hair.

"You want it heated and with ice cream?"

"Oh, yeah, baby. You know what I like." He says it like she offered him sex.

The waitress sighs, and now I know Piss Hair is not her boyfriend.

I eat my soup while she prepares their pie. The guy sitting across from Piss Hair is thin and wiry, and he clearly thinks everything Piss Hair says and does is awesome. I shall call him Fanboy. After the waitress fills their coffee cups and gives them their pie, Piss Hair slaps her on the fanny.

"Thanks, sugar."

She grips the handle of the coffeepot tight enough to make her knuckles whiten. For a moment, I think she's going to bash it into his face or pour it over his head, but she doesn't. She walks back behind the counter.

Piss Hair is clearly pleased with himself. Fanboy is actually bouncing on the seat. He is so hot for Piss Hair right now. This could be very convenient for me. Piss Hair winks at me. He's seen me watching and wants to see if he can pull me into their game.

I look at him through hooded eyes and give him a slow smile and a little shot of pheromone. He licks his lips. This is going to be easy. Hard to get is clearly Piss Hair's favorite, so I ignore him and finish eating.

The waitress brings me some more Coke. She looks like she wants to tell me something, but then she doesn't. She seems like the sort who has volumes to say but never says any of it. Her sad face reminds me of my mother. I look over, and Fanboy is making rude gestures as part of a litany of things he'd like to do to either the waitress or me—I'm not sure which. Maybe both, but it's all for show. He really wants Piss Hair, but he won't ever admit that. The waitress's silence and Fanboy's desperation are making me edgy. I want something to happen.

The men finish their pie.

As they walk out, Piss Hair leans over and whispers into my ear, "Feel free to come out to the truck and join us in a little fun."

Ah, just the invitation I need. One of the lamest things about being a succubus is that I can't ever ask for sex. I can flirt, I can use pheromones, and I can even touch to a certain extent. But I have to be invited before I take someone's soul. If I didn't have to be invited, I could just take the soul of any man I could get in my grasp. That's what all the human literature says we do, anyway, but that's not what happens. We have to be invited, and so do incubi.

After the guys leave, the waitress buses their table. She holds up a couple of one-dollar bills.

"A two-dollar tip on a thirty-six-dollar tab. Assholes."

I smile sympathetically at her. Don't worry. I'm going to go eat them now. I leave the money for my meal on the counter, and I tip extra.

It's a nice night. The air is clear and crisp, and the moon is a bright pale sliver in the sky as I walk over to the eighteen-wheelers with their convenient sleeper cabs. The pit inside me feels like it's roaring. I always feel like that when I've targeted someone. I haven't touched Piss Hair yet, but I don't think that'll be a problem. They're standing outside having a smoke.

Fanboy nudges Piss Hair when he sees me. He's bouncing on the balls of his feet. Fanboy is a spaz. Piss Hair, though, tries to play it cool and just nods at me, but I can tell he's surprised to see me.

"Hey, guys," I say.

"Hey yourself. You lookin' for a little fun?"

"Well, you know what they say. Two heads are better than one."

"Oh, I've got some head for you," Piss Hair says, grabbing my hand and pressing it against his crotch.

I'll give him this—unless there's a sock in there, he's hung like a horse.

"Nice," I say.

"Me first and then my friend," Piss Hair says. "He likes my sloppy seconds."

"I'm sure he does, but I'm really looking for a little two-on-one action."

Fanboy looks like he's ready to burst he's so excited.

Piss Hair raises his eyebrows. "Well, I'm all about making sure a lady gets what she wants."

Fanboy opens the door into the back of the sleeper cab and climbs inside. He's got his pants down and his dick in his hand before Piss Hair and I even make it inside.

"This is so hot," he says.

It's so not. The truck smells like a locker room.

"Slow down there, tiger," I say. "Wait for us."

Piss Hair stays behind me and starts kissing my neck while he peels up my tank top. I press back into him and make appropriate moaning noises. He pulls my jeans down, and I wriggle out of them. I've recently decided to go commando when I'm hunting to speed things up, and I skip the bra for enticement and speed. Just like everyone else, I try to be as efficient as possible at work.

"Get her ready for me," Piss Hair instructs Fanboy, who flips over onto his back and slides under us.

That's unusual in these situations, but what Fanboy really wants is a reason to nuzzle his buddy. Whatever. One of the convenient things about being a demon is I can turn my head around three hundred sixty degrees. This comes in handy, because once Piss Hair is inside me, I turn my head around, latch on to his lips, and suck his soul out. One down. He slumps against the door.

Fanboy pauses. "You done already, man?"

"I'm that good," I say in a purr. "Why don't you clean me up down there, and then you can take a turn."

"All right!" he says and enthusiastically resumes.

I lean over and suck his soul out through his dick. Since his mouth is covered, there's no hope of his soul slipping away. Two souls in one night. Life is good.

I get dressed and look at the two bodies. I decide to give Fanboy in death what he could never truly have in life. It takes some effort, but I'm much stronger than I used to be. I strip them both and then curl Piss Hair around Fanboy so that they're spooning. I look out the cab window. A few more vehicles have parked, but I don't see anyone around. I slip out of the truck and back into the night, but almost instantly, the hair on the back of my neck stands on end. I close the truck door just enough to make the light go off but not enough to latch it. Crouching down, I look through the parking lot. I don't smell anyone. I don't see anyone, but... hold on... there are disembodied shadows against the building. It looks like three men, and at least one of them is holding something that casts a shadow like the biggest gun I've ever seen. It's cartoonishly large. I scan the parking lot, trying to locate them, but I still see nothing. Okay, to cast a shadow, they have to be between the building and a light, and the only light is a lone streetlamp at the edge of the parking lot. I don't understand why I can't see them. It doesn't matter, though. I know where they are.

Crouching low, I roll under the truck, so I'm now between Piss Hair's truck and what I assume is Fanboy's truck. I pop up between them, and as quietly as possible, I sprint to the end of the trailer. I can see my car parked behind the truck stop, but I would have to cross about thirty feet of unprotected ground before the building would give me some cover. I can still see the shadows on the building. They haven't moved. Shit.

I try to push back my panic and focus on what I should do right here, right now. I consider switching to my true form because I'm faster when I'm not wasting energy looking human, but it's difficult to maneuver car keys with my claws. Plus, I'm too big to fit in my car as a demon, so I would have to use precious seconds switching back at the car. It's too risky. All of this is too risky. What do these guys want from me? How are they tracking me? How are they invisible? Why won't they just go away? Crap. I crouch down like an Olympic runner and prepare to sprint across the parking lot, but I don't move. I'm paralyzed with fear. I can't exactly be killed with bullets, but I can be injured—and the shadow of that gun looks awfully big and nasty. What if it's not a regular gun? What if it's some kind of succubus-killing gun? I'm freaking out. I think about my mother and what she would do if I was killed. Then, just to make myself crazy, I think of all the guys I've killed and wonder what that was like for their families. A wave of guilt hits me, but I still don't want to die.

I feel like I've been crouching here for hours, but I know it's only been a minute. A car pulls into the parking lot between the streetlight and the building. As the shadows disperse, I see my chance and run for it. I run as fast as I can. I've already got my keys in my hand, and as I reach my car, I hear someone shout, "It's on the move!"

I open the door and throw myself inside. The rear window shatters but without the sound of gunfire. They must have silencers on their weapons. Slamming the door closed behind me, I put the keys into the ignition and start the car. I can hear heavy footfalls, like people running in boots, but I still can't see anyone. I throw the car into reverse and peel out of the parking space as a bullet shatters the driver's-side mirror. Staying low in the seat, I barely look as I shift into drive and burn through the parking lot like a bat out of hell. My heart is pounding, and my pulse is throbbing as I speed up the access road and onto the ramp for 95. Shit, shit, shit.

When I finally calm down enough to ease up on the gas pedal, I slow down to sixty-five miles per hour and fish around for my phone. I speed-dial Ian.

"This is an unprecedented amount of communication from you, Cupcake," he answers.

"Someone just tried to kill me." Saying it out loud somehow makes it worse. "I need to see you."

"Don't come here. Meet me at the pickup."

Chapter 6: Help!

The pickup is where I'm supposed to meet Ian every week to drop off souls. Though I almost never meet him there, I still know where it is—an abandoned building in Southeast DC that hasn't been redeveloped yet. I know Ian is going to take two of my souls, but I don't know where else to turn.

Details from tonight play over and over in my head. I run through every point, trying to find clues to who might be after me and why. Unfortunately, I've got nothing as I pull into on-street parking. When I get out of the car, I don't get a watched feeling, so I guess the shadow men didn't follow me. Instinctively, I make myself look vulnerable, hunching my shoulders and shuffling my feet. If I get lucky, someone might jump me and I can take his soul. But the street is empty. All the cretins must be taking the night off.

I squeeze through a broken doorway in the back of the building, and my eyes immediately adjust to the dark (another bonus of being a demon is really good night vision). I see Ian pacing in the center of what was probably once a showroom. He's in human form, but he's chosen a big one—well over six feet tall and looking like one of those big Hawaiian wrestlers. As is typical, he's in full character.

"Where you been, bitch?" I think Ian must have been a frustrated actor in his former life.

"I was in Maryland."

"I don't like to wait."

I roll my eyes and stick my hand into my mouth to give him a couple of my souls.

"Stop," he says. "You're going to need them." His voice has changed back to his regular, more eloquent tone.

What? Ian is turning down souls? Suddenly, I'm very frightened. "Why?"

He doesn't answer. "Tell me what happened tonight."

I explain about the shadow men and how I figured out where they were.

Ian nods and starts pacing again. "I've asked around, but no one seems to know this group."

"This group? Exactly how many groups are trying to kill me?"

Ian shakes his head. "Such a narcissist. It's not about you, Cupcake. There are always groups trying to kill demons."

"Like who?"

"Well, there are certain priests drawn to demon killing."

"Priests?"

"Sure. Priests, witch doctors, certain physicists, and the occasional yokel."

"Wait, did you say physicists?"

Ian smiles and arches an eyebrow.

What the hell is he saying, and why are all those people hunting demons?

"Look, it sounds like a lot of people hunting us, but in reality, it's only a handful. Witch doctors don't even exist in the United States. Well... there might've been a few in New Orleans, but like everyone else in that city, they were devastated by Katrina. The Catholics no longer officially support things like exorcism, and the yokels have never been dangerous."

"And the physicists?"

"Are seeking proof of our existence."

"Why?"

"Because of quantum physics. Look, Cupcake, we don't have time for all this. Right now, I'm primarily concerned that someone is after my harem. I haven't had contact from one of my girls in over a week, and unlike you, she never makes me go looking for her."

"What should I do?" I can't believe this is happening. As if being turned into a demon wasn't bad enough, I also can't believe Ian refers to us as his harem. Gross.

He writes something on a sticky note and hands it to me. It's the address for a hotel in Falls Church.

"Are you serious? I can't afford a hotel."

"You can't afford to go home. Go book a room. I know a guy there. Don't leave the hotel, and wait for me to contact you." He pulls a roll of bills out of his pocket, peels off several hundreds, and hands them to me. "Tell the night clerk that Ian sent you, and give me your cell phone."

"Why?" I don't like this. I don't like this at all.

"They might be using it to track you."

"How am I supposed to tell my mom I'm not coming home for a while?"

"Don't. That'll provide them with clues and potentially endanger your mother."

I hand him my phone. "But how am I supposed—"

He throws up his hand to stop me. "You're a big bad demon now, Cupcake. You can't always tell your mommy everything you're doing. When you get close to the hotel, park your car somewhere else and walk the rest of the way." He starts for the door in long purposeful strides. "If you value your mother's life or yours, you'll keep your mouth shut. Now do what I told you."

He yanks open the door I had to squeeze through and slams it behind him, splintering it into a dozen pieces.

I stand there for a moment after he's gone. Despite the fact that I have three souls rolling around in my belly, I feel empty in a whole new way.

Chapter 7: Hell's Hotel

It doesn't take long to get to Falls Church at this time of night, and the hotel is right on Route 50. It looks like it might have been part of a budget chain at some point, but now it's an indie place called Besties. I park the car in a nearby neighborhood, grab the bag of clothes that I keep in the trunk for disguises, and walk to the hotel. The night clerk looks barely alive.

"Hi," I say as I approach the counter. "I need a room. Ian sent me."

His eyes widen at the mention of Ian's name. "Not a problem." He hands me a key card but doesn't ask my name. "That'll be a hundred dollars."

I hand him one of Ian's hundreds.

The clerk looks at me very purposefully. "I hope you enjoy your stay."

"Thanks."

I don't like the way he's looking at me. It's a very weird look. It's not sexual. Sexual is my bread and butter. No, it's... I don't know, pitying somehow. He gives me the creeps, and he smells funny, but I can't quite put my finger on why.

My room is on the second floor and not nearly as nice as the Jerk's room at the Ritz, but it's clean and, I hope, safe. The décor is done in neutrals: taupe walls and tan-and-brown bedspreads, and there's a generic abstract painting over the bed. The bathroom is the color of standard-issue filing cabinets, but at least it has basic toiletries. It also has an enormous mirror that covers the wall across from the shower. I look like hell. My hair is a mess. There are smudges on my tank top, and dirt from the truck-stop parking lot is ground into the knees of my jeans. I take off my clothes and start washing them in the sink. I'm not sure how long I'm going to have to stay here, so I need all my clothes. When that's done, I hang them in the shower to dry. Naked, I look at my reflection again. On impulse, I shift to succubus.

Unlike Ian's, my skin is a pastel-pink color. My claws aren't black like his—they're white, but they're still thick and sharp. I don't have long impressive horns like Ian either. Mine are just little nubs. I wonder if the differences are gender based or age based or just demon genetics. Do demons have genetics? What the hell am I now, and why would a physicist care? I so want more information on that. I liked physics in high school and did well in it. I was planning on taking more physics classes in college but never got the chance.

I resume my human form—my original human form: straight blond hair, blue eyes, average height, broad shoulders, slender hips, average breasts. I don't know what Ian saw in me. Why me? Did I do something to bring this on myself, or does he just pick girls at random? I have to admit I'm really curious about the rest of his succubi. I wonder whether they're like me or if they know more. The whole situation has gotten so weird, as if it wasn't weird enough to begin with. My mom must be worried sick.

With a heavy heart, I finally go to bed.

I wake up a monster again. This is getting to be a habit. Trying not to think about the ramifications of that, I hit the shower. Taking a shower in demon form is much more satisfying than taking one in human form. In human form, it feels like I'm showering in a very thin plastic bag. It's weird, but I always do it that way at home for fear that Mom will walk in. *Mom.* She must be beside herself with worry. I need to figure out a way to get a message to her without the shadow men knowing. My soul stomach is fairly full, but my actual stomach is empty. It's hard to formulate secret plans on an empty stomach. Also, coffee would help.

Ian told me not to leave the hotel, but he didn't say I had to stay in my room. Luckily, the hotel has a restaurant. I shift back into a human, put on the least revealing clothes in my bag, and go down for breakfast: three eggs sunny-side up and a rare steak. This is another change since becoming a succubus. I prefer my food as raw as possible, with the exception of chicken soup. I used to be the opposite—one of those people who ordered her steak well done and made everyone else at the table groan. Now, truth be told, I'd be happy if they didn't cook it at all, but you can't really order raw meat in a restaurant, with the exception of sushi. Well, there is steak tartare, but hardly any restaurants serve that, and the ones that do charge a fortune. Too bad they don't have it here, since I'm on Ian's dime.

After breakfast and five cups of coffee, I feel clearheaded enough to tackle the mom problem. I know five cups sounds like a lot, but caffeine and alcohol don't affect me like they used to.

Walking through the hotel lobby, I spy the obvious answer to my situation. A circular rack by the reservation desk holds a small selection of cards. Technology is a wonderful thing, but sometimes, old-school is the way to go. I buy a birthday card. It's not Mom's birthday, but who cares. I quickly write, *Happy birthday, Mom. I love you.* Addressing it to her work should throw the shadow guys off, although I'd never felt them around my house. Better safe than sorry.

The same dough-faced, creepy guy is working the reservation desk.

"Doesn't anyone else work here?" I ask, trying to be warm and friendly. But this guy is a heat sink for that kind of thing.

He gives me a wry smile. "I'm working a double today."

"Could you do me a favor? Could you mail this for me?" I hand him the card.

He looks at it like it might be a letter bomb. "I guess."

"Great." I start to leave and then remember something else. "Hey, could you mail it from someplace that isn't here?"

"Sure, I live out in Manassas. I'll mail it from there."

He gives me a knowing look that sends a chill through me. It's a pleasure to go back to my room just to get away from that guy. I don't know what it is about him, but he makes my skin crawl.

On the way to my room, I notice a tall woman and two young men walking ahead of me. There is something familiar about them, but I can't place it. As I get closer, I figure it out: they stink of demon. I stop and watch as they go into their room down the hall. The woman is statuesque and beautiful, and the two men are so handsome they're pretty. One of them is a bushy-haired blond with a deep tan. He looks like the quintessential surfer. The other has black hair and piercing blue eyes. They are both very solicitous of the woman. They're carrying her luggage. Surfer Boy opens the door, while Blue Eyes ushers her inside. Surfer Boy looks around and spots me staring at them. He snarls at me before going into the room. He slams the door shut behind him. Demons. What the hell kind of hotel is this?

I go back into my room, but there's not a lot to do besides watch TV. I'm bored with that almost immediately, and my mind starts to wander. I think about when I met Ian the first time. He looked like a nice college guy then. The weird thing about my relationship with Ian was that there was nothing weird about it. We went to the movies. We talked for hours. We played cards with my friends. He even made me dinner. We dated for three intense weeks before we slept together. And then he stole my soul. Men suck. And now so do I. I chuckle at my own joke. Man, I'm bored.

Unable to sit around any longer, I wander into the halls and down to the lobby, which is surprisingly busy. There are women everywhere. Most of them are alone, but some of them are accompanied by men, sometimes several men. Everyone looks like they just stepped out of a magazine ad, except no one appears to be happy. Behind the counter,

Creepy Guy is handing out key cards as fast as he can. He spots me coming into the lobby.

"Go back to your room," he shouts at me. "You've already got a key."

Two of the women begin snarling at each other.

"Ladies, ladies, calm down," Creepy Guy shouts.

The whole lobby reeks of demon funk. Then it dawns on me who these women are. They are Ian's harem—them, me, the whole demonic lot of us. Holy crap! I start backing out of the room. Several of the women are snarling now. Something base in me, something deep in my fight-or-flight zone, screams at me to run, so I do, as fast as I can, back to my room.

I slam the door behind me and lean over with my hands on my knees, trying to catch my breath. That was horrible. Demons do not belong together in large numbers. We can barely tolerate one another in small numbers. What was Ian thinking, gathering us all here? Is he crazy?

I flop onto the bed and turn on the TV. I don't care how boring it is. I'm not leaving this room until Ian shows up and tells me it's safe.

A couple of mind-numbing hours later, after having been told how to decorate my house, lose weight, and invest in real estate, there is a knock on my door. I look through the peephole to find Creepy Guy standing there.

I open it a crack. "Yes?"

"Ian requests your presence in the Jefferson Room right now. Here is your seating assignment." He thrusts a ticket through the gap.

Looking at the slip of paper, I step into the hall. "Seating assignment?"

"Yes, please proceed to the Jefferson Room, and do not deviate from your seating assignment."

Creepy Guy seems very serious. Although for him, serious is almost lively.

"Okay, fine. I'll be there in a minute."

I close the door and put on my shoes. What fresh hell is this?

Chapter 8: Bored Meeting

So, I go down to the Jefferson Room, which turns out to be the hotel basement. It's full of folding chairs. My little slip of paper reads *Red 5*. Several of the women from the lobby are already there. None of them are sitting anywhere near one another, but the room still stinks of agitated demon. I'm feeling agitated myself as I find the row of chairs marked with a piece of red construction paper and sit in seat 5. It feels remarkably like kindergarten, if kindergarten were in hell. This better be good. I want some information, and then I want to get out of here. Why did he have to pile all of us in here together? It's stifling.

At least it's an opportunity to see the other succubi. Ian certainly has diverse taste. Assuming all the women are in their original forms, which is admittedly a pretty big assumption, there are all shapes, sizes, and ethnicities in the room. More and more women arrive every few minutes. Finally, some of the men start arriving. They're accompanying the same women as before, and they all take their seats toward the front. I'm not certain what the men are doing here. They're definitely demons, but are they incubi? If so, what are they doing in a meeting called by Ian? So far as I know, incubi don't do the gay thing, so I don't understand their connection to him. Demons are definitely the solitary type. For instance, no one turns to look at anyone coming in. No one speaks to anyone else. The only reason I can see so much is that the red section is in the back. It looks like the place is full to me, or at least demon-full. The women are evenly spaced throughout the room. The men are seated around the women they came in with. To add anyone else would crowd someone. There are twenty-seven women in the room and eleven men.

Ian picks this moment to appear. He's wearing a suit and tie today—he looks like a corporate type. Maybe this is our annual meeting. I wonder if there will be a PowerPoint presentation with charts and graphs depicting deaths and acquisitions. Maybe there will be bonuses. Souls for everyone, yay! Instead, Ian clears his throat and adjusts his tie.

"I know you must be wondering why I've called you all together in this unprecedented gathering. I assure you it is as uncomfortable for me as it is for all of you."

A subtle shifting occurs among the women.

"However," Ian continues. "I felt time was of the essence, so speaking to all of you individually seemed impractical. Sugar Pie is missing, and Cupcake was attacked but managed to escape. We are all in danger."

That stirred the crowd. The women who have men with them start whispering to them. Wait a minute. Did he just call me Cupcake like it's my name? The fuck? I thought that was just a term of endearment. I figured he called all his girls Cupcake. Ian is a freak.

He holds up his hands. "Settle down." The murmuring stops. "Let me see a show of hands of anyone who has been followed in recent weeks."

Three other women raise their hands.

Ian calls on them and asks them to tell him their stories. They sound similar to mine in the sense that they all had the feeling of being followed, but they couldn't see or smell anyone. None of them, however, had actually been attacked. I guess I'm just lucky that way.

"Okay," Ian says when the last woman is finished talking. "Then I think it's reasonable to assume that Sugar Pie has been captured or killed and that the rest of us are in extreme danger."

One of the women up front, one of the ones who have men with them, raises her hand. "It seems to me someone is attacking your harem, which begs the question of why I am here, since I haven't been part of your harem in years."

Ian nods. "Listen, Snickerdoodle, I asked you, Honey Bun, and Sugar Muffin here because I thought it would be shortsighted to assume that just because you were out of the harem, you were safe. If someone is coming after me, you may be in danger too."

"Why would someone come after you?" the woman up front asks.

"Well, that's the big question, isn't it?" Ian says. "Why indeed? We need intelligence. We need to know who these people are and what they're after."

One of the women in the middle of the room raises her hand.

Ian calls on her. "Yes, Pumpkin?"

"How do you know it's people? Couldn't it just be another incubus horning in on your turf? The Mid-Atlantic is a pretty big piece of the pie. Maybe someone wants a bite."

Ian shakes his head. "Cupcake saw men's shadows, men with guns. Demons don't carry guns. Besides, another incubus would bring it directly to me. There's no gain in capturing or killing Sugar Pie. To want my spot is to want my harem."

All of this is confusing the hell out of me. "Mid-Atlantic region" makes it sound like he's some kind of regional manager. I'm starting to think a PowerPoint is going to be in this meeting after all. Not to mention, how could another incubus take his harem? How would that even work? I have a sudden desire to see an organizational chart. Do demons have those? Why does everyone else in the room seem to understand all this? Did I miss a memo?

The succubus Ian called Snickerdoodle stands, and three men stand with her. "I'm taking my harem and leaving. I'm unconvinced that this has anything to do with me, Ian. Good luck with your problem."

"Snickerdoodle, sit back down!" Ian commands in his best deep demon voice, but she and the men ignore him and continue out of the ballroom.

The two other succubi who came in with men also leave. Ian is clearly furious at their departure.

"Fools!" he shouts after them.

Personally, I'm just happy to have fewer demons in the room. Also, I'm very curious about the fact that those succubi had incubi harems, but they used to be part of Ian's harem. How does that work? For me, the goal has always been to get my soul back, but clearly, these women didn't do that. Did they pay off Ian and then branch out on their own, or did he release them from their contracts for some reason? Why doesn't this demon stuff come with a manual? I have a lot of questions.

Ian glowers at the rest of us. Since all of us are still part of his harem, we can't really leave without his permission. I hope he's going to tell us the plan soon, because this whole situation is freaking me out.

Sadly, Ian doesn't appear to have a plan. He keeps pacing back and forth at the front of the room, grumbling and growling to himself. Everyone starts to fidget. I begin to count the stripes on the gold-on-gold wallpaper to keep myself awake. It's not as easy as it sounds. The stripes are very faint, and I keep losing my place.

Finally, someone in the middle of the room raises her hand.

Ian practically pounces on her. "Yes? What is it?"

"What are we supposed to do?"

At first, he looks like he's going to rip her head off, but then he seems to pull himself together. "Gather souls. Gather as many as you can and bring them to me as soon as you get them. I need to be as powerful as possible if they're coming after me. Now go!"

Gather souls? That's his solution? What a load of crap. Not to mention the last time I checked, no one was even following him. This is very disheartening. The other girls start to file out of the room. I linger because I don't know what to do. Ian notices and walks toward me.

"Go on, Cupcake."

"Go where? There are people trying to kill me."

Ian sighs and pulls that big wad of cash out of his pocket again, peels off a few more hundreds, and hands them to me. "Hang out here a couple more days. If I find out anything, I'll let you know. Otherwise, you're on your own."

"What does that mean? Are you cutting me loose? Does that mean I get my soul back?"

He shakes his head. "Why do you even want that? Didn't you see that poor slob in the lobby? Seven thousand is the magic number, Cupcake. That doesn't change."

"But if you're cutting me loose—"

"I haven't done anything. Don't anticipate. I was hoping the girls would know more and could help. You're such a baby that I thought there was a good chance you were missing something." He stretched and stared up at the ballroom ceiling as though the answer might be written on the tiles. "I need to work on this some more. Just stay here. I'll be in touch."

He walks away with his hands in his pockets and his head hung low in a very unnerving way. Ian has shown me a lot of faces, but until today, worry has never been one of them.

My legs feel like jelly as I walk back to my room. I haven't been this scared since Ian turned me into a succubus in the first place. As I pass through the lobby, I notice Creepy Guy is still behind the counter. I guess he's the "poor slob" Ian was referring to. Does that mean this guy got his soul back? I stand there watching him for a moment.

He must feel me looking at him, because he looks up. "May I help you?"

I approach the counter. "I'm going to be staying a few more days."

"Okay."

The obvious thing to do at this point is to go back to my room, but my feet feel glued to the floor.

"Is there anything else?"

"How long have you known Ian?"

Creepy Guy's eyes narrow, and suddenly, he seems less creepy and more dangerous. "A very long time." The way he says it indicates the conversation is over.

"Great."

For some reason, I wave at him before going back to my room. Fantastic. Here is a guy who could really have information for me, and I'm waving at him like an idiot.

Chapter 9: The Barback

My stomach starts growling. And despite the three souls I'm currently carrying, my soul stomach is hungry too. Instead of going back to my room, I head to the hotel restaurant. It's a Mexican-themed restaurant, but the menu is so bland it bears little or no resemblance to actual Mexican food. I assume the only way it can stay open in this ethnically diverse area is because it's attached to a hotel. Regardless, they have chicken tortilla soup on the menu. It's not my mother's chicken soup, but it'll do in a pinch.

I sit at the bar and eat my soup. The guy working barback is way too old for the job. He's stringy thin, his clothes hang off him like they were bought for someone else, and he's sweating profusely. It's cold in the restaurant, so I'm guessing he's jonesing for a fix. I know I'm not supposed to do this, but I'm jonesing for my own fix. When I hear him tell the bartender he's taking a cigarette break, I pay my tab. Instead of going back to my room, I slip out through a door that leads to the back parking lot. There he is, smoking in the small square of light cast by the open door.

I ask him if I can bum a cigarette, and from there, I do what I do best. I know I shouldn't eat so close to where I'm staying, but I'm hungry, and his soul gives me a warm satisfied feeling as I go back to my empty hotel room.

There's a show about whales on TV, so I watch that until I fall asleep.

A knock on the door wakes me. The clock says it's two a.m. I'm in monster mode, so I quickly assume human form and check the peephole. It's Creepy Guy again. If Ian is having another meeting, I'm going to kill him. Creepy Guy knocks again, and I open up.

He steps into the room uninvited and closes the door behind him. This makes me edgy and uncomfortable. I don't know what this guy's deal is, but I don't like him, and I don't want him in my room.

"Don't do that again," he says.

"What?"

"Don't eat someone on premises. Do it again, and you're out. Understand? I don't care if you do belong to Ian. That's absolutely not allowed."

How the hell did he know I ate someone?

"Sorry," I mumble, and he's gone before I can say anything more coherent.

Out of curiosity, I pull back the heavy curtains and look out my window. There are flashing red and blue lights all over the back parking lot. This is the first time I've seen the aftermath of my behavior, and it seems like a lot of people for one scrawny dead guy. When the paramedics wheel the stretcher with his body on it into the ambulance, I feel a pang of guilt. Did the guy have a family? Was he finally getting himself clean after years of using? Was that why he was holding down a job? I shake it off.

I can't lament every meal. It'll make me crazy. I don't contemplate the life of cows and chickens after I eat them, and like it or not, men are just meals now. I close the curtains and go back to bed.

I wake sweating and panicked from a nightmare in which all the men I've killed were chasing me and demanding their souls back. I look down and see my giant white claws and start to cry. I hate being a demon. I'm sick of killing other people to survive. I hate it. A big tear rolls down my cheek and lands on the bedspread, where it promptly eats a hole through the fabric.

Whoa.

Now, on top of everything else, I have acid tears. Fantastic.

I miss my mom.

After a shower, I head down to the hotel restaurant for breakfast. Everyone is talking about the dead guy, and I feel terrible. He was well-liked. They miss him. I'm a horrible monster. And yet, I'm hungry—not just food hungry but soul hungry. I feel like I'm two people: I'm Alma and Cupcake, and I hate it. This is all Ian's fault. I'm a monster because of him, and he can't even protect me from whoever is chasing me. He's a big red loser. I have an overwhelming urge to roar, and it's all I can do to hold it back.

Returning to my room seems like a horrible idea. I can't bear the thought of hanging out all day, watching TV. I'm bored, restless, and hungry. I'm used to hunting all night and sleeping most of the day. I'm off my normal schedule, and it's making me antsy. I've got to get out of this hotel. What's the point in staying? Ian obviously doesn't know what he's doing, so I'm on my own anyway. Creepy Guy knows I killed the barback, and who knows how he might use that against me? That seals it. I'm leaving.

I go to my room and quickly pack my things. It doesn't take long before I'm back in the lobby, turning in my key to a nice woman. I don't know where Creepy Guy is, but I'm glad he's not working. I get the feeling he might give me grief if he were here.

On the walk to my car, I try to decide what to do. Should I go home? Will that endanger Mom? I don't know. I need some clothes, and I need to tell her I'm going to be gone awhile. I decide to risk it. After all, home is the one place I've never sensed that I was being followed.

It's a beautiful day, and the drive to my house is pleasant with weirdly light traffic. It doesn't seem like the sort of day to run away from home because someone is trying to kill me. Mom's car is in the driveway when I pull in. This must be her week to do night auditing. I don't even make it to the front door before she's running out of the house in her robe.

"Alma!" She hugs me so tight I can't say anything. "Where have you been? I've been worried sick!"

"It's okay, Mom." I realize I haven't considered the lie I need to tell to cover where I've been. Stupid. I stall for time. "Let's go in."

She walks inside with me, but the minute the door is closed, she folds her arms across her chest and fixes me with the mom stare. There is no escaping its power. I decide not to stray too far from the truth for fear that her lie detector might be extra sensitive because of my long absence.

"Where have you been?" she repeats.

"You know that guy Ian that I used to date?" I say as I walk toward my room.

She follows, but at least she can't see my face this way.

"Sure. I never liked him. He was nice but in that too-nice way."

Which, boys and girls, brings us to the moral of the story—always listen to your mother.

"He was all right, Mom."

He so wasn't, but for the purposes of the lie, I need him to be.

This is greeted with only silence, which is the closest my mother ever comes to telling anyone that they're wrong. Arguing with my mother can be very unsatisfying. I empty my bag into the hamper in the hall and continue to my room.

"I ran into him at the gas station, and he was going camping. He invited me along, so I went."

I let her fill in the rest of the story in her head. I'm sure it goes something like this: he offered me drugs and I couldn't resist, so I've been holed up with him in a tent, blowing dope and having sex. I came home when the drugs ran out.

"Why did you send me that crazy birthday card at work instead of calling me and telling me you were going to be gone for a few days?"

"I'm sorry, Mom." I say without looking at her. "My cell phone died, and he was leaving right then. The gas station had birthday cards, so I just got one and mailed it when we stopped at the grocery store in Manassas."

She shook her head. "Why didn't you use Ian's phone?"

Good question. "Oh, he has this thing where he doesn't bring any technology when he's camping. You know how guys are. It makes him feel all manly. Like he's roughing it."

"It sounds irresponsible to me."

Did you catch that? Ian is irresponsible for not having a cell phone. I'm not irresponsible for letting my battery die or for running off for days without telling her. See what I mean about unsatisfying arguments?

"Yeah, I guess it is, but what could I do?"

"I still don't understand why you sent the card to work instead of here."

"Wasn't it more fun to get it at work? I thought it would be fun."

That could be the dumbest fucking thing I've ever said, but Mom, being Mom, accepts it.

"It was nice to hear from you."

This twists in my gut. I'm a horrible daughter. On the other hand, I'm a soul-sucking demon. It's a miracle I'm any sort of daughter at all.

"Look, I'm really tired. I'm going to take a nap, and then I'm going to meet Ian later. He wants to go to the shore for a while, and I think I'll go with him."

The disappointment immediately registers on her face. "Well, if that's what you want to do..." She just sort of wanders back down the hall.

Oh good, more guilt to enjoy while I pack.

Chapter 10: Stan

I throw my bag in my trunk and then realize that camping gear might not be such a bad idea after all. Ian's money isn't going to last too long if I'm renting hotel rooms.

The garage is stuffy and dark and full of all manner of crap. Really, everything is in there but the car. It takes me a while, but I locate the camping gear and start pulling it off the shelf. Mom appears in the doorway. She's dressed for work now.

"I thought Ian had camping gear?"

"It's never a bad idea to have extra stuff," I say. "If it rains or something, it's good to have an extra tent."

"That tent probably leaks now," Mom says. "We haven't used it since before your father died." She's clearly very upset with me. She would never invoke my father if she wasn't. "He loved that tent," she says wistfully.

"If you don't want me to take it—"

"No, no. He'd be happy it was being used."

This sucks. I hate that I have to leave her and can't tell her why. I drag all the gear to the front of the garage. It's no easy feat, thanks to all the crap in the way. Mom follows me around as I pull it all out and stuff it into my trunk. She doesn't say anything. She just lingers like a shadow. It makes me crazy sometimes how passive she can be, but since I became a succubus, her passivity has made my life a lot easier, so I shouldn't complain. Hunger for souls is already starting to gnaw at me. I'm going to have to hunt soon, and it needs to be far away from here.

I kiss Mom's cheek. "I love you, Mom."

"I love you, too, Alma."

Driving away is one of the hardest things I've ever done.

Interstate 66 toward Shenandoah turns out to be far more typical of Northern Virginia traffic than my drive home was this morning. A wreck between a Chevy and a Subaru snarls traffic for miles, and I sit in frustrated silence with a million of my neighbors waiting for it to clear. The radio does little to distract me as I try not to think too hard about my predicament. The thing that weighs heaviest on my mind right now is my soul issue. I should be feeling pretty good. Instead, I feel like I've lost souls. Have I used them up? Is that how it works? Ian was never very clear on how the soul thing worked. He just said take souls, and when you have three, give me two. He never said much after that. Obviously, the whole demon thing is much more complicated than I thought. Ian always calls me a baby, and I'm starting to think he's right about that. I'm over my head here, and I need some guidance. Unfortunately, we demons seem to be like reptiles dropped into the world to fend for ourselves with little or no support. Since he turned me into a succubus last year, Ian has hardly been a font of information.

The scenery around Front Royal is beautiful, but I'm so hungry that much of the beauty is lost on me. Before I get onto Skyline Drive, I stop at a little country store to buy several cans of a type of chicken soup that doesn't require added water, a can opener, and some fuel for my camp stove. The sales clerk looks at me funny as I pile the cans of soup onto the counter.

"You must really like chicken soup."

I consider eating him for stating the obvious. Instead, I shake it off and grumble an affirmative. It comes out a little more like a growl than I would prefer.

He's clearly startled by my response and rings everything up as quickly as possible. "Here you go." Wide-eyed, he hands me the bag.

"Thanks."

Traffic is light on the parkway, but I drive the speed limit because I don't want any attention from the police. Sadly, the speed limit is really slow, and I'm gritting my teeth by the time I reach the campground.

Lewis Mountain is the best campsite. My father always said so when we came here when I was a kid. It's got the fewest campsites of all the campgrounds in the park, and I'm thinking the more privacy, the better.

Pulling the tent out of its bag, I'm hit with the smell of stale reefer, a reminder of why Dad always wanted privacy. I sigh at the memory of my father. He wasn't much of an earner, but he was a good cook, handy around the house, and really fun to play with. I miss him, and the smell of reefer fills me with nostalgia. If only he'd stuck to pot, he might still be alive today, but alas, the siren song of heroin eventually pulled him away.

I set up the tent, noting how stiff the fabric is as I stretch it over the rods. Mom was probably right—if it rains tonight, this thing will leak like a sieve. Drowning in childhood memories and aching for the souls of men, I open a can of chicken soup and drink it cold out of the can before climbing into the tent to sleep for the rest of the day.

I wake up just after dark. Bugs are singing, and somewhere, an owl is hooting—the night seems to call to me. I would stretch, but I'm back in demon form, and I take up the entire tent. I could be mistaken, because let's face it, even a three-person tent is pretty small, but I think I'm getting bigger. That's not good. In demon form, I'm already over six feet tall, with broad shoulders and an even broader belly, which is plenty big enough. The first time I saw my true form in the mirror, I was terrified, but it's weird what you can get used to. My human self is pretty short, so after I got over the shock of transformation, I really enjoyed the height. Sometimes, when the house was empty, I'd transform just to get things off the top shelf. It was kind of awesome. Right now, though, it's a little inconvenient. I switch back to my human form so I can maneuver around the tent.

It's six miles to Big Meadows Lodge from here. I debate whether I should walk in hopes of snagging someone on the trail or drive to give myself the most time in the lodge looking for company. I decide to drive. Pulling someone off the trail has a myriad of risks that I'd prefer to avoid—not to mention if I'm being followed, I'd rather have the safety of my car and a quick escape nearby. The drive to the lodge only takes a few minutes, and I find a parking spot in a dark back corner of the lot in case I need to eat in my car.

The lodge is the same mix of stone and wood clapboard that I remember. We never stayed in the lodge, but at least once during a trip, we would eat dinner there. I can hear the live entertainment as I walk in. I hope some lonely campers have come to listen to the music. Oh, please, let there be lonely campers. I sit around for over an hour, sipping beer and listening to the music and people talking around me, waiting for an opportunity. Unfortunately, the room is full of couples and a few families. Not what I need. Finally, just as I'm about ready to go roam the trails, a single guy walks in. He isn't wearing a ring, and there's no scent of a woman on him. Smiling at me, he takes the stool next to mine at the bar. Bingo!

Here's the rotten part. This guy starts talking. He's chatting me up but not in a slimy way. He works for the OMB in DC and is taking his first vacation in three years. I don't ask what OMB stands for. I don't want to know. I don't want to know anything about him, but I can't seem to get him to shut up and just get on with it. The pressure of his job and life in the city is getting to him. He's originally from rural Arkansas, but he doesn't have any family left down there, so he decided to take two weeks in the Shenandoah to hike and clear his head. I figure he's pushing forty. He has wavy brown hair graying at the temples and warm brown eyes that seem tired and kind. He's pleasant, easy to talk to, and not bad-looking. The thing is I like him, but I'm starving, and no other prospects have walked in. It's close to closing time, so I touch his hand, put on my sincere face, and let him take me back to his campsite. His name is Stan.

I feel every bit the monster when I leave his tent. Despite the enormous healthy soul rolling around in my belly, I feel lower than I have in a long time. Right now, I feel like someone should capture me and put me out of my misery. Or at least, I feel that way right up until the net falls over me and there's a stinging pain in my neck. I don't even get a chance to fight before someone puts a bag over my head. I can't move. It's like my whole body has gone numb. I know I'm being dragged through the forest, but I can't really feel it. It's the strangest sensation, until it isn't.

Chapter 11: Captured

When I wake, the dark is so perfect that even I can't see in it. I'm curled into a ball, and my back is killing me. Unfortunately, stretching is impossible. Wherever I am, I'm shoved in here pretty tight. Then I realize I'm in demon form. I switch back to human, which gives me considerably more wiggle room. And I'm naked. This is not good. I've been sleeping naked since I became a succubus because I have a tendency to destroy pajamas when I turn into a demon while I'm sleeping. Now am I better off as a naked human or a naked demon? Well, since they've already captured me, I'm guessing they aren't going to be scared off by the demon thing. I decide to capitalize on the cute, scared girl thing and see if that gets me anywhere. Making myself as waiflike as possible, I curl up into a ball in the corner of the box I'm in and wait. A strong breeze is blowing in on me, so at least I don't feel like I'm suffocating.

It's hard to tell time in a place like this. There are no visual clues. My mind starts to drift. There's no telling how long I've been in here, except I still have that big fat soul in my gut, so it can't have been too long. I'm contemplating crawling around to figure out more of my surroundings when I hear a door open and voices talking, but I still can't see anything. I listen intently with my super demon hearing, hoping to find something out about my situation.

"I don't like this," a male voice with an ambiguous accent says.

"You don't have to stay," another male voice says, but this one definitely sounds foreign, melodic. I guess he's Caribbean or maybe from one of the African countries.

"What are you going to do with her?" the first voice asks.

I still can't place his accent. It seems like a blend, like maybe he's lived all over the world.

"Don't ask questions you already know the answer to," the second voice says.

I'm almost positive he's African now. I'm not too good at picking out regional African accents, but he has that French lilt, so I'm thinking one of the former colonies.

"The last one was a catastrophe. And how do you propose to feed her?"

Ambiguous Guy seems pretty upset.

"I've got that worked out."

African Guy seems really confident, and I'm not sure whose side I should be on. I'm hoping one of them wants to let me go, because then I would definitely be on that guy's side.

"Worked out how?" Ambiguous Guy insists.

"Do you really want to know those kinds of details? I think you're better off not knowing."

Okay, so African Guy is in charge.

"Do you want to talk to her or not?"

"No. I think this is a bad idea."

There's a pause when no one says anything. I start to think they've left.

"Oh, all right. I'll look at her."

"Good. You'll see. She's perfect."

African Guy thinks I'm perfect. I'd be flattered if I knew for what.

The lights come on but not brilliantly. The room is bathed in red light. A door at the other end of the room opens, and two men walk in. I'm in a box about the size of a toilet stall. The front of it is clear plastic with holes cut into it, which is where the breeze is coming from. I wonder how strong the plastic is. I'll test all of it as soon as they leave.

"Here she is," African Guy says. He's the proverbial tall, dark, and handsome. He's about six feet tall, with ebony skin and handsome features. He's wearing an expensive suit but no tie. His white shirt glows in the red light.

Next to him stands the ambiguous-accent guy, who is dressed like a Catholic priest. What the hell?

"Has she spoken?" he asks.

"Not yet. She just woke up a few minutes ago. See how she's transformed herself, though? She's all doe-eyed to make herself seem meek and vulnerable. How great is that? She's much better at this kind of transformation than the last one, and she's much younger."

The priest rubs his chin. "Hmm. I see that. I don't know, Sefu. This is straying pretty far from the charter."

So, African Guy's name is Sefu. Okay, Sefu, what the hell are you up to, and what does it have to do with me?

"Peter, please. I'm not concerned about charters. I want to make a real difference here. Isn't that the ultimate goal of science? To make the world a better place."

Peter nods, but his eyes show more concern than agreement. I consider trying to reach them with pheromones through the holes in the thick plastic, but with the fans blowing, I don't think that will work. This is very frustrating and more than a little scary.

"When are you going to bring her into the unit?"

"Later today, after the suits are finished."

"What?" Peter asks.

"They had to be fitted with filters now that we know about the pheromones. We don't want another incident."

I don't like Sefu.

"Ah, poor Jenkins," Peter says.

"At least the other one was never taken into the unit."

"Thank God," Peter says.

Sefu arches an eyebrow at him.

"You know what I mean." Peter still looks very concerned.

I assume they're talking about the succubus Ian called Sugar Pie. It sounds like she's dead—possibly starved to death—but apparently, she took one of them with her. Good for Sugar Pie, but I don't want to die. I wonder what I have to do to survive around here. I wish these two would talk to me instead of about me.

Sefu looks at his watch. "We should go."

They leave without saying anything else, and the room returns to pitch-black. I take the opportunity of their absence to run my fingers over every inch of my cell, transforming back into a demon to reach the top. The whole place seems to be poured plastic of some sort. I can't feel any seams, and with the exception of the few holes in the front with air blowing in, I can't feel anything that would indicate a way out. I test the strength of the wall with the holes, figuring it would be the weakest. It might be, but even at full demon strength, I can't crack it. I test the other walls, the ceiling, and the floor, just to be certain there isn't a weak point, but I don't find one. How did they get me in here? It's like they poured it around me. I miss the light.

Chapter 12: Goons

The light comes back on and wakes me. It sounds like someone is coming down the hall. I shift back into my human form in an attempt to look nonthreatening. I don't know how much time has passed, but two guys in what look like space suits designed by medieval knights have come in with a wheelchair. One of them also has a huge, weird-looking gun that looks like the gun that cast the shadow at the truck stop.

"Step back from the door, please," says the guy with the gun. His voice is filtered and sounds metallic, like a robot's.

Assuming the plastic wall nearest them is somehow the door, I crawl to the opposite side. The other guy uses a key card against a plate on the opposite wall. A red light goes all the way around the front of the cell, but it's too bright for me to see where it's coming from. Are they seriously using a laser to get me out of here? The plastic in front of me slides up. I don't understand how I didn't feel the seams last night. Gun Guy has his big gun leveled at me, so I'm compliant.

The other guy hands me a white hospital gown. "Put this on, please, and sit in the wheelchair."

I do as I'm told. I don't like it, but that gun scares me. I can still remember the way I felt when they captured me, and I'd like not to feel that again. Gun Guy walks behind us as the other guy pushes me down the hall. It's bizarre. I'm being treated like a patient. All kinds of medical horrors go through my head. What if they want to dissect me? What if they're going to conduct Mengele-style experiments on me?

My heart is pounding by the time we stop. I'm so panicked that I'm having trouble controlling my form.

A nondescript white door is opened, and the two guys take positions on either side of it.

"Go in," says Gun Guy.

The office is large and ornately decorated. One wall is covered in mahogany bookshelves full of books on things like medicine, religion, the occult, and physics. Physics again. What the hell? The other wall is covered in African masks, but I don't know enough about African art to know which country they're from. There is another low bookshelf, and on top of it are a couple of handwoven baskets. The large desk is also mahogany. On top of it sit a new laptop, a phone, and an abstract soapstone carving. In front of the desk are two leather chairs. No one else is in the room, but then another door that was made to look like part of the wall opens, and Sefu walks in.

"Take a seat, Alma," he says cordially, as if we get together like this all the time.

It freaks me out that he knows my name, but I sit down. He's not wearing a special suit, which worries me. What is he that he isn't worried about sitting in the same room with a succubus? To test the waters, I shoot a little pheromone at him. He smiles.

"That's cute," he says. "And clever. It's always good to test the waters and see what you're dealing with, but your scent has no effect on me, so don't bother."

Well, it was worth a try.

"I suppose you're wondering why you're here."

"That would be nice to know, yes. More importantly, when can I leave?" I figure in for a penny, in for a pound.

Sefu steeples his fingers. "Well, that's a bit more complicated. Let's start with why you're here."

"Okay." Did I mention I don't like this guy?

"I've been watching you for quite some time, Alma, and I think you might fit in here nicely."

"'Here' being the hospital?"

He chuckles at that. "In a manner of speaking."

"Where am I?"

"Baltimore."

Oh, hell no. "Look, I'm from Northern Virginia. We don't do Maryland. I'd like to go home now."

He smiles at me again. I'd love to suck that smile right off his handsome face.

"As I said. I've been watching you. In particular, I've been watching you feed and noting how you make your choices."

Well, that's just creepy. I don't say anything.

"It seems to me that you show a predilection for choosing men who are about to die anyway, or at least men with risk factors for dying. Failing that, you seem to choose men who are unpleasant."

"Assholes."

He might be all eloquence and dulcet tones, but I don't see why I should be.

He smiles again. "Yes. Until your last feed. Why him?"

"Desperation. Sometimes, I don't have good choices, so I have to take what's available." It's weird to be talking about this to someone, but he obviously already knows what I do, so there's no point in trying to hide it.

"Interesting. Does that bother you?"

"Killing someone? Of course it does. Wouldn't it bother you?"

He nods. "Most definitely. When you were human, were you a vegetarian?"

"No."

"So you make a distinction between humans and animals?"

"Yes." I don't like this line of questioning. It's making me uncomfortable. After all, I've justified meals that way.

"What do you consider yourself?"

"I don't know what you mean." Now I really don't like this line of questioning.

"Are you a human or an animal?"

I don't know how to answer that. Is it a trick question? If I say I'm an animal, does it give him permission to kill me? "Neither, but I'd like to be human again."

"So you don't feel human now?"

I can't see any advantage in not answering truthfully. "I try to be human as much as I can, but let's face it—we both know I'm not anymore."

"True." He taps his fingers together, which is smug and irritating.

"Look, it's obvious you already know what I am. Why all the questions?"

"It's important to know what you think about what you are. How we see ourselves is critical to how we interact with the world."

Sefu has some deep thoughts, great. How does that get me out of here?

He looks at me for a long time. Silence grows heavy in the room, but I'm patient, and I'm not going to break it.

Finally, he says, "If you were given the opportunity to have steady access to the souls of men who were already dying, would you accept that over hunting?"

"You want me to have sex with dying men? What kind of pervert are you?" I grimace at him.

"You've had sex with lots of dying men." He arches an eyebrow at me. "What kind of pervert are you?"

Asshole. I'd like to have sex with him. "The men I've slept with weren't in the hospital on their deathbeds. I doubt most of the guys dying in this building are going to ask me to get it on with them, no matter how hot I am."

He laughs at that.

Great. He thinks I'm funny.

"You have some very arcane ideas about your abilities."

Arcane? "What?"

"You seem to cling to medieval standards of demon behavior. That's charming but pointless."

I have no idea what he's talking about. "I don't understand."

"I can see that."

He smiles again. His teeth are startlingly white against his dark skin. It's a combination I'd find beautiful if he wasn't so irritating.

"I've given you a great deal to think about. You should ponder it."

He doesn't seem to do anything, but the two goons who brought me in suddenly appear with the wheelchair again.

"Our guest needs to go to her room for a while."

Oh, shit. He's sending me back to the box. I have a little wave of panic. I don't want to sit in the dark in that little cage again. My fight-or-flight kicks in hard, but one of the goons still has that big, shiny gun, so I push back the demon in me. Alma has a better chance of getting out of here than Cupcake does. I wish I could see the goons' faces, touch them, but they're covered head to toe in protective clothing. I wonder how tough the fabric is and whether my claws could rip through it. Let's hope it doesn't come to that.

I meekly sit in the wheelchair and try to appear as gentle as a lamb, but my senses are in high gear as they wheel me down the long hall. They aren't taking me out the same way they brought me in. It could be an attempt to disorient me in the endless white hallways, but I don't disorient easily. My nose tells me this is a very different hall—the chemical smells are different. I tuck all the smells away, cataloging them in a mental map for later if I get a chance to escape.

Chapter 13: The White Room

The wheelchair stops at a door marked with an infectious-disease logo. Gun Guy taps in the passcode, and the other goon rolls me in. It's the whitest room I've ever seen: walls, floor, ceiling, bed linens—even the metal bed frame is painted white.

"This is your room," Gun Goon says. "If you need anything, we're just outside."

His actual message is loud and clear—*if you try to escape, I'll shoot you.* I hear the lock on the door engage when they leave.

I didn't notice it at first, but the room has a tiny bathroom with a shower, toilet, and sink. The only splash of color in the entire place is the hygiene products they've left me: soap, toothpaste, a toothbrush, deodorant, mouthwash, shampoo, and a hairbrush. They're all sitting out on the small vanity with a plastic drinking cup and some towels. It's like I'm staying in a freakishly clean, really scary hotel. I've got to get out of here.

I start looking for openings of any kind, but there's nothing—not even any visible air vents. The realization makes me instantly claustrophobic. A windowless room without an air vent strikes me as a death trap. Even the door is so tightly fitted it barely registers as being there. I try to calm down and consider my options, but I don't have a lot of them. It occurs to me that they are probably watching me. To distract myself from impending suffocation, I start looking for cameras. Despite combing every inch of the room and furnishings, I can't find any. That doesn't dissuade me from thinking that they're watching me; I just can't figure out how they're doing it. And of course the ceiling in this room is at least fourteen feet high. Even standing on the bed in demon form, I can't reach the light fixture. The camera must be in there.

Frustrated, I shrink back into my human form and sit on the bed. There is nothing to read in here and no TV. It's like the worst hospital room ever. I'm not even sleepy, so I don't have much to do except contemplate Sefu's offer. I'm curious about his statement that I have medieval sensibilities and arcane ideas about my abilities. What does that mean, exactly? Was Ian bullshitting me when he gave me the rules? If so, were all the rules fake or only some of them? I know one thing—I'm starting to have a gnawing hunger around the edge of what I think of as my soul stomach. It's not a huge problem right this minute, but I don't want to end up like Sugar Pie. Crap. I don't know what to do. Maybe it's best to go along with Sefu until I have an opportunity to escape. I'm certainly not going to escape from this room. They've got this place locked down tighter than Fort Knox. I'm just about ready to ask one of the guards if I can talk to Sefu when there is a knock on my door, and the priest comes in.

He's not wearing a protective suit, and he smiles at me. "Hi. I'm sorry to intrude."

That's rich, like this whole situation isn't one giant intrusion. I just stare at him.

"My name is Peter," he says. "I'd like to talk to you for a few minutes if you don't mind."

This guy is a lunatic. I almost thought he was going to say he'd like to talk to me about my Lord and Savior, but apparently, he's not evangelizing today. On the other hand, it's not like I have any other options for conversation at the moment.

"Go ahead."

"I'd like to discuss souls with you."

I guess he's on the other end of the soul business. He tries to save them. I try to eat them. "Aren't you afraid to be in here with me?"

He smiles that little smile again, where the corners of his mouth just barely lift. "No."

His self-confidence irritates me. I'm tempted to shoot him with a load of pheromones, but I restrain myself. I shouldn't waste the energy, and it's not like I can eat him here anyway.

"Can you tell me something?"

The smile again. "Maybe."

"What happened to Sugar Pie?"

"Excuse me?" he says and looks legitimately confused.

I guess she didn't go by Ian's pet name with them. "The other succubus."

He shakes his head and puts on a sad face. It looks sincere, but some people are naturally good actors.

"She died," he says.

He doesn't smell like he's lying, but I don't trust him. I nod and try to push back my panic. I knew she was dead, but somehow, hearing him say it makes it more terrifying.

"We were uncertain as to her feeding requirements. It was our fault. It's one of the reasons we made sure you fed just before we captured you."

"Feeding requirements" makes it sound like I'm a new species at the zoo. Which I guess I am. I lean against the wall and fold my arms across my chest.

"I believe Sefu has made you an offer to provide you adequate food."

"Yeah. As a priest, doesn't that bother you?"

He does the little smile again. I'm starting to think it's a nervous habit. "Not really. Souls are more complex than we once thought."

"How so?"

"Let me ask you this." He rubs his hands together, obviously warming to his topic. "What do you think a soul is?"

I think back to the handful of times I went to Sunday school as a kid. "I always thought they were like a little piece of God inside of us."

He raises his eyebrows in surprise. "So you think you're a god-eater?"

I shake my head. "Nothing that grandiose. I get hungry. I eat. No god involved."

"Hmmm." He paces around a bit. "How much do you know about physics?"

"Some. I took it in high school."

"Are you familiar with the law of conservation of energy?"

"Sure, it's the first law of thermodynamics."

This time, I get a real smile, almost a grin. "Souls are energy," he says with unconcealed excitement in his voice. "To eat a soul is to convert its energy, not to destroy it. You can't destroy it." His eyes light up with excitement.

"Great," I say. "So I'm not doing anything wrong."

The smile disappears. "I wouldn't say that, but I doubt you're quite the monster you think you are." He heads for the door.

"Who said I think I'm a monster?"

He stops with his hand on the doorknob. Without turning to look at me, he says, "Don't you?"

The door closes behind him. I think I like him even less than Sefu.

Chapter 14: Ebola Man

They leave me alone for a long time. I pace. I rest. I even sleep some. I'm not sure how much time passes. Each minute I'm awake seems like an eternity, and my hunger grows. I'm starting to think they've forgotten about me when there's a knock on the door. A gurney is rolled in by two guys in hazmat suits. One of them is Sefu.

The guy on the gurney looks bad. He looks half-dead already, although I'm not sure from what. His eyes are completely bloodshot, and he seems to be bleeding in a lot of places.

"This is an advanced case of Ebola. He was brought directly here from a container ship that's now quarantined in the harbor. He has at most a couple of hours to live, likely less. Make your choice," Sefu says.

This guy looks bad. I don't want to touch him. I don't want to be breathing the same air as him.

"Isn't he contagious?" I ask.

"Very," says Sefu. "To humans."

I'm not normally squeamish, but I have to admit I'm having trouble with this.

"You need only kiss him," Sefu says.

I look at him, and our eyes lock. I'm not sure what I expect from him, but what I get is hard to explain. I can't say I trust him exactly, but there is some strength for me. I lean over and kiss Ebola Guy. I do it as gently as I can while still extracting his soul, which is warm and filling. He looks at me when I stand back up. You won't believe this, but there is gratitude in his eyes as he dies. A shiver runs down my spine as they wheel him away.

They lock the door behind them, and once again, I'm stuck in my white prison cell. The impact of what I've just done hits me hard. I try to blow it off. It's convenient, I tell myself, like delivery. But I feel sick despite the warm, full soul in my belly. This is not how I was told to do things. I was told I had to work for it—not only to hunt but also to offer up my body for what I was receiving. A kind of tit for tat, so to speak. It feels wrong in a whole new way to kill a man without giving him sex in return. To simply lean over and suck out someone's soul goes against everything Ian taught me. Ebola Guy's soul didn't try to slip away either. Maybe it was because he was so close to death, or maybe it was because Ian lied about souls being slippery. I wonder what else he lied about. Curiosity eases my conscience long enough for me to fall asleep.

I've hardly dozed off before I wake from a horrible dream: I'd been walking through the hospital, stopping in every room and stealing the souls of all the sleeping people. I grew bigger and bigger until I had to crawl to get down the hall, but I kept taking souls. I wake in a cold sweat in monster form, which scares the hell out of me. I switch back to my human shape and get out from under the damp sheets. I pace around, desperate for a way out of here, but there isn't one. I don't know how long I've been here or whether it's day or night. This whole situation is making me crazy. I throw myself against the wall in desperation and pound as hard as I can. Nothing happens. I slide down the wall until I'm huddled in a ball on the floor and crying. I've got to get out of here.

Sefu comes in without bothering to knock first. He stares at me sitting on the floor, and I see a look of disgust cross his face before he schools his features back into something more neutral. I'm sure I look a fright. I've been crying for what feels like hours but was probably more like minutes. There are little holes burned into my hospital gown and pits in the floor from where my acid tears landed. I glare at him and go into the bathroom and wash my face. I run a brush through my hair before facing him again.

"You sit around in your human form. Why is that? Isn't it more comfortable to be in your true form?"

"Demon form is not my true form," I say indignantly. "My demon form was forced on me. My human form is my true form."

This seems to please him, although not enough to make him smile.

"Why have you been crying? Didn't you like the soul I provided?"

"It felt wrong to do that."

He scowls at me. "Wrong? You, who've cut down men in the prime of their lives, think it's wrong to eat the soul of a man on death's door. Did you not see the look of relief on his face when you took away his not-inconsiderable pain? Do you not see that as a kindness?"

He has a point. I know he has a point, but it still felt wrong—more wrong, somehow. I don't know. All of this is confusing.

I shake my head. "That was hunting. They could run. They could've not hit on me. They got to have sex before I took their souls. It was more of an exchange than just taking."

"You are a hypocrite. You have pheromones to make them want you. You have scent glands in your fingers so that if you touch them, you can track them down even if they slip away. And as for sex in exchange for their souls, I like sex as much as the next man but not enough to die for it. Given that you don't explain the true nature of the transaction, that hardly seems like a fair exchange." He sticks his finger in my face. "You need to wake up to the reality of what you are and where you are and decide how you're going to survive. Are you going to cling to pointless, medieval laws, or are you going to do the human thing and make the best of a horrible situation?" He stares at me for a moment. "I'll leave you to deliberate."

Chapter 15: Situational Ethics

I don't know what to think. I pace and stare at the white walls. My mind feels as blank as the paint all around me. I don't know how to feel. I don't know what to do. I can't figure a way out of this. I wonder if this is what happened to Sugar Pie. I wish I knew her real name. More and more, I'm starting to worry that she and I are going to share the same fate. Frustrated, I sit at the head of the bed and lean against the wall.

I must have dozed off, because a knock on the door wakes me. I don't bother to get up. What's the point? Father Peter comes in and surprises me by sitting on the other end of the bed.

"Sefu tells me you're having a hard time feeding."

That makes me sound like a baby who can't latch on. "Oh, no," I say sarcastically. "It was great. Like delivery, only alive."

He wipes imaginary lint from the knee of his black pants. "Barely alive."

"So that makes it okay? Seriously?"

He shakes his head. "No. But there are degrees of how bad something is. There is such a thing as making the best of a bad situation."

"Your congregation must love you." I laugh, but it's a fake laugh. "Situational ethics are so much easier than the usual Catholic do-this-not-that approach."

He smiles at me. "I don't have a congregation. I'm not that kind of priest. You're a lot brighter than the last succubus."

I'm suddenly offended on Sugar Pie's behalf. "An IQ test isn't exactly required to get this job."

He cocks his head at me. "What is required?"

I look away from him. "Oh, it's a lengthy process. Kind of like getting a job with the feds but more complicated. The competition is fierce."

He sighs. "Now you're just making stuff up. Why don't you tell me the truth?"

I'm sick of this guy with his soft voice and his little-boy smiles. I get off the bed and start pacing.

"Why should I tell you the truth? What about a little truth from you? What am I doing here? What do you want with me? How long do you plan on keeping me? Will you kill me like you killed Sugar Pie?"

"We didn't kill Sugar Pie." He cocks his head again. "Was that her name?"

"In a manner of speaking."

"Well, we didn't kill her, at least not intentionally. She died because we didn't know how to feed her. We didn't understand that the soul feeding was actually necessary to sustain you. We thought it was something you could do, but we didn't understand it was critical for survival."

What a moron. "Why on earth would we take other people's souls if we didn't have to in order to survive?"

Peter nods and looks at me apologetically. "That's a very good point. Why indeed?"

"Didn't Sugar Pie explain it?"

He shakes his head. "No. She wouldn't speak to us. She stayed in demon form the whole time and pounded on the walls and clawed them to try to get out."

"Then how do you know about the pheromones and scent glands?"

He frowns and doesn't say anything.

Then it dawns on me. "Oh, autopsy." I'm suddenly sick to my stomach. I back away from him and cover my mouth, trying not to vomit.

Father Peter holds his hands out to me. "It wasn't like that, Alma. We know those things from observing her when she killed Jenkins."

I'm not sure why, but him using my real name makes me snap. I instantly go from angry to furious. Who do these people think they are? I'm not the only monster here. My control slips so quickly that I'm not sure who is more shocked by the transformation. My roar is thundering.

Armed guards spill into the room, big guns drawn.

"Wait, wait!" Father Peter shouts, holding up his hands and standing between the guards and me. "Alma," he says over his shoulder. "Please pull yourself together."

A sense of self-preservation helps me to rein in the beast and shrink back to my normal form.

The guards lower their weapons but don't leave.

"It's all right," Peter says. "It's fine, just a misunderstanding. Please, wait outside."

They hesitate, but slowly, they leave the room. I can't see their faces beneath their hazmat helmets, but I can feel them glaring at me.

Peter turns back around. He's visibly shaken. "Look, I know this is not an ideal situation for you, but try to see the bigger picture. Having the opportunity to study you will advance science in ways we probably can't even imagine yet. You are a quantum creature. Do you realize the implications of that? You don't abide by the laws of Newtonian physics, and yet you live in a Newtonian world. The ramifications are mind-boggling. No wonder earlier generations thought demons were magic."

I don't want to be a quantum creature. I never asked for this. I just want him to go away. "So I'm trapped here, eating the souls of mostly dead men, until what? You're done studying me? Then what?"

He shakes his head. "I'm not in charge of the study, but I can tell you this—Sefu is not a bad man. He comes across a bit harsh, but he truly wants to bring about positive change in the world. He's a visionary."

I can't help thinking of all the people who've been ground under the heels of visionaries throughout history. "Great."

"Think about it, Alma," he says as he turns to leave.

"Think about it." That makes it sound like I have a choice, but really, these guys have given me the same "choice" Ian did when he turned me into a succubus to begin with—deal with it or die. That's a Hobson's choice, not a real one.

I lie across the bed and stare at the ceiling, waiting for sleep to come. I still don't understand how this is supposed to work. Sefu and the priest keep speaking in generalities, and no one has said specifically what "studying" me will entail. And what about eating? Are they just going to find excuses to bring dying men to wherever it is we are? Won't people notice after a while that all the guys brought here leave dead? That plan isn't going to work for very long.

I fall asleep trying to figure out what my future is going to look like. Nothing I consider looks good.

Chapter 16: Work Permit

Because there is no clock in my room, I don't know how much later it is when Sefu comes in. Again, he doesn't knock. I wake with him staring at me from across the room. I'm in demon form, but the moment I see him, I revert to human.

"Do you always shift into demon to sleep?"

I sit up and rearrange the hospital gown. It's tied very loosely at the neck and not at all in the back so that I don't destroy it when I transform. "No. I always go to sleep human and wake up demon."

He stares at me with eyes so dark brown they're almost black. It feels like he can see right through me.

"You told me before that being a demon was forced on you. How did that happen?"

I'm torn. I don't have warm, fuzzy feelings about Ian, but I'm not sure I want these guys to get their hands on him either. "Poor choice in boyfriends."

"One of your boyfriends turned you into a demon?"

"'Boyfriend' is really too strong of a word. It was more just this guy I picked up. Becoming a demon is kind of like contracting an STD."

I'm not sure why I lie. I guess I don't want to seem like a dupe. If he knows I had an actual relationship with Ian, he'll press me for more details about it. I'm not ready to divulge the whole truth or, at least, as much of the truth as I know, which lately, doesn't seem like a lot.

"Are you saying you never saw him again?" He narrows his eyes at me.

He knows I'm lying or, at least, not telling the whole truth. I don't say anything.

"If that's true, then how did you know you were a demon?"

"The pink skin and claws were good clues."

He smiles. It's a warm smile, a mature smile, not like Peter's nervous smile. "How did you know what to do? Did you instinctively know how to capture souls?"

"No, I just reread *The Confessions of St. Augustine*." This gets me a bona fide laugh.

"You are clever," he says, nodding at me. "You are also a liar, but given the circumstances, I suppose that's understandable."

I'm careful to keep my expression neutral and don't say anything.

"I think that you are exactly what I've been looking for. You are a survivor, Alma. More than that, you're practical and resourceful. So here's what I'm going to do: I'm going to give you a little freedom. I'm going to give you some clothes and a badge—several badges, actually—and I'm going to send you to specific rooms at specific times to feed. Once you've acquired the soul, you're going to call a code blue, and then you're going to blur your features and retreat as the code team comes in. There's so much chaos around a code that it won't be difficult, especially for someone of your talents. When you're not feeding, we're going to be testing you. I want to see the extent of your abilities. If you can manage to do all this without a fuss and without trying to escape, I'll let you see your mother. I'll give you a legitimate job here at the hospital, where she can actually call you. More than that, if you play along, I promise that, eventually, I will bring meaning to this horrible thing that was forced on you. What do you say?"

Two things get to me as he's speaking. The first is the possibility of seeing my mother. The second is that he'll kill me if I say no.

"Okay," I say. "Deal."

He leaves, and I lie back down. I don't see a way around his offer, but an opportunity might present itself later for me to get out of here. I fall asleep thinking about possibilities.

I wake to a knock on my door. One of the suited goons comes in with a stack of clothes, some shoes, and a badge.

"Knock when you're dressed," he says and leaves, closing the door behind him.

The clothes are a plain white bra and panties, black socks, cheap black tennis shoes, jeans, a white T-shirt, and a long gray vest with pockets. The badge is for Mary Johnson, who works for the hospital cleaning service. As I get dressed, I stare at her face. I wonder who she actually is and where they got the picture. By the time I slip on the vest, I've transformed myself into Mary Johnson. I check the bathroom mirror to make sure I've got her face right. I do. Showtime! I knock on the door, and two goons escort me to an elevator at the opposite end of the hall from my room. Sefu is waiting there, standing next to a cart with cleaning supplies and a big garbage can on it.

"Go to room 314 and help Oscar Winston. Make good choices."

The elevator doors open with a chime. Sefu waves me ahead of him, and I roll the cart in. He steps in and uses a key before hitting the lobby button.

"There is another bank of elevators when you reach the lobby. Take those to the third floor."

I nod. He steps out, and the doors close behind him.

I'm alone in the elevator. My heart is pounding as the elevator ascends. I look to see which floor I started on. With the exception of the large lobby button, there are eight other buttons. Six of them are marked with a *P* followed by a number. There are four additional buttons at the bottom without markings, and they require a key to push. None of the buttons lights up, and there is no panel at the top of the doors indicating which floors I'm passing, but it's taking a while to get to the lobby, so I'm guessing I was pretty deep.

When I reach the lobby, I roll the cart off the elevator. The sunlight streaming through the front windows of the hospital stops me cold. I have no idea how long it's been since I've seen the sun, but it's a comforting sight. It's all I can do to quell the urge to run through the front doors and into the daylight. There are random men standing in the lobby. I can smell the tension on them, and it's not because they're worried about loved ones in the hospital. They're worried about me making a run for it. I'm not sure what they could do in front of all these people, but uncertainty makes me cautious.

I force myself to roll the cart to the opposite side of the lobby to the other bank of elevators. It only takes a minute to reach the third floor, but my palms are sweating. There is a nurses' station in the middle of the floor, and no one gives me a second glance as I roll my cart to room 314. An old man lies alone in the room. There are several machines hooked to him, and they're all chugging and chirping along. I'm not ready for this. I give myself some time by actually emptying the trash can in his room. There isn't much in it—some wrappings for various medical paraphernalia and a couple of tissues. Something about that makes me sad. There are no cards in the room, no flowers. This guy is all alone in the world. I look at him again and realize I recognize him. It's Oscar from the Ritz, the one the Jerk gave such a hard time. Suddenly, I feel like the worst kind of hypocrite. I was going to eat this guy's soul when he was having a drink at the Ritz, and only the Jerk showing up prevented me from doing so. But now that the old guy is here, on death's door, I'm squeamish? Disgusted with myself, I check the door to make sure no one is passing by before I lean over and kiss him. His soul slips out with barely any effort on my part. He never wakes up. When the machine next to him signals a flatline, I hit the big red button behind his head. I roll my cart into the hall as a couple of nurses hurry toward the room, and I hear the intercom system calling a code blue in room 314. As the nurses pass me, I tell them I hit the button when his machine went off. They nod at me, barely registering what I said, as they rush to help Oscar. But Oscar is beyond help.

I roll my cart slowly back to the elevator. Walking past the entrance doors in the lobby is even harder the second time. I want out of this place so badly. The problem is I don't know how they tracked me, and I can't safely leave without knowing how they found me. Dejected, I roll the cart to the special elevator. When the doors open, two men in hazmat suits are waiting for me.

Chapter 17: Weights and Measures

"Follow us, please," says a filtered voice. "You can leave the cart here."

I follow them around the corner, where one of them touches a panel on what looks like a concrete wall. A hidden door opens to reveal a set of stairs. The hazmat guys and I descend into a familiar white hallway. They escort me to my room and lock me in.

The room looks different. A heavy white plastic chest of drawers sits in one corner. A clock hangs over the door now, and a calendar is stuck to the back of the door with a magnet. The best thing, though, is that on top of the dresser there are two *Smithsonian* magazines, a copy of the *Baltimore Sun*, and a paperback mystery. It's still a prison, but at least it's a prison with stuff to read. Apparently, if you're a good little monster, you get treats.

I take a look at the chest of drawers. There are two little drawers on top. One is empty, and the other contains nine identification badges—all for cleaning-crew members. All of the women pictured look different from one another. Various ages and races are represented. The implication of all these badges hits me pretty hard. Sighing, I put them back and close the drawer. The rest of the drawers just have more clothes. I take the newspaper and lie across the bed to read. I may as well take the opportunity while I have it. If it's today's paper, I've been in here for two days. Funny, it seems like a lot longer. Meanwhile, my stomach is growling—not my soul stomach, my real stomach. Getting a soul diminishes what I need to eat, but I still need to eat a little. Why the hell haven't they offered me a meal?

It doesn't take long to finish the paper. I'm about to start on the magazines when Sefu walks in.

"You did a nice job today," he says. "You were quick and efficient and drew no attention to yourself."

I don't respond. It's not like it was my plan or anything. I ate a dying man's soul, hardly a significant accomplishment for a succubus.

"Do you have any questions?"

"Yes. Can I get something to eat?"

He frowns at me. "You just ate." There is a hint of a threat in his voice.

"I can't survive on souls alone. I need real food too." I can tell from his expression that this is unexpected news.

"What would you like?"

"Do you have any chicken soup?"

He looks at me like I've asked for something rare and exotic. "I'll see what I can do," he says and leaves.

Half an hour later, there is another knock on the door, and Father Peter enters with a tray of food. It's hospital food, complete with the little plastic covers over the bowls.

"The closest thing they had to what you asked for was cream of chicken soup. I wasn't sure how much you needed, so I brought you three." He actually seems apologetic. What a weird guy.

I take the lid off the first soup and drink it from the little plastic bowl. There's also cherry gelatin and hot tea. "What is this? A liquid diet?"

Father Peter gives me that quirky smile of his. "Actually, yes."

Great. I'm eating like an invalid. At least I shouldn't gain weight this way, although that hasn't really been an issue since I became a demon.

"After you eat, I'd like to take some measurements, if you don't mind."

If I don't mind. That's rich. I love how he talks like I'm a guest at his house instead of a prisoner trapped in this bizarre institution.

"Sure," I say, all butterflies and sunshine.

"I'd like to compare your original height and weight against your demon form's height and weight."

Although I haven't ever thought to do that, I have to admit the idea intrigues me. "Okay."

Father Peter pulls a little notebook out of his jacket pocket. It seems a little low-tech for this place. "How much did you weigh before you became a demon?"

I try to think. "I'm not sure. One hundred twentyish."

"Okay. Have you checked your weight since then?"

"Not that I recall." Somehow, knowing my exact weight hasn't been high on my list of priorities.

"How tall were you?"

"Five foot five."

"Okay, then," he says. "Let's go take some measurements."

I'm not sure what I thought was going to happen. I guess something involving a mark on the wall and a bathroom scale. Clearly, I was wrong. He leads me out of the room and down the hall. Two goons follow us at a less-than-discreet distance. One of them has the big gun. Super. As we walk, I look at the priest and realize I've been giving him some deference because of the collar, and I'm not even Catholic. I resolve to drop the "Father" when I talk to him. He's not my father, and he's not my priest. He's my captor.

We turn the corner into yet another long white hallway. What is it with these people and white? Would a splash of color kill them? We reach a door, and he leans into a scanner so it can scan his eye. So much for low-tech.

The door opens, and we enter a room with a lot of equipment in it. I don't even know what most of it does. He leads me over to one wall where there is a large three-sided chamber. "Go ahead and step on the scale," he tells me.

I step onto the metal floor of the chamber and feel it shift slightly under my weight.

"How you look now, is that your original form?"

"Yeah." Okay, I make my breasts slightly larger these days and my belly slightly flatter, but he doesn't need to know that.

"Oh, that's interesting," he says.

"What?"

"You weigh one hundred forty-two kilograms."

"What's that in American?"

He lets out a soft snort. "Roughly three hundred thirteen pounds."

"Seriously? What the hell?"

"This is a very accurate scale. Close your eyes."

I close my eyes, and a moment later, he tells me to open them again. "You're five feet, four and three-quarter inches."

"Okay. Why do I weigh so much?"

"I'm not sure. It would seem to be a conservation of mass issue. Could you transform into a demon now?"

"Um, I don't want to mess up my clothes."

Clearly, this hasn't occurred to him.

"Oh, okay. Well, just take your clothes off first." He turns his back.

Yeah, you heard me. He turns his back to a woman who can transform into a demon. No matter how fast the hazmat guys get in here, they can't get in faster than I can kill him. I know he knows that, and yet he still turns his back to give me privacy. What a lunatic. I slip out of my clothes and toss them onto the floor outside the chamber. Then I let myself relax, and ta-da! I'm a demon.

"Okay," I say in my deeper demon voice.

Peter turns around, and his eyes widen, which is funny because he's seen me do this before. He pulls himself together quickly and checks the monitor.

"Ah, as I suspected. Your weight hasn't changed despite the fact that you are now six feet, seven inches tall."

That's sounds impressive, but I'm a little demon. Ian is way bigger in his demon form than I am. Although sometimes he's bigger than others, which makes me think he can adjust his demon form just like he does his human form. I can't do that. When I'm a demon, I'm always this size.

"Interesting," Peter continues. "You're a closed system."

"What else would I be?" It's weird to hear myself speaking in my demon voice.

He shrugs. "We weren't sure if you were able to somehow shift part of your mass into a different dimension."

I roll my eyes at him. "Someone's been reading too much science fiction." Then I realize how ridiculous that must sound, coming from a big pink demon.

"Can you step out here for a minute?" he asks.

I step out of the chamber, and he takes his time walking around me. It's unnerving.

"Hmm," he mutters. "Odd."

> So much about this is odd that it's hard to imagine which odd thing he's referring to. "What?"

"You don't seem to have any sexual characteristics in this form. Are you intentionally masking them?"

The question takes me off guard. "No."

"How do demons reproduce, then?"

I suddenly feel like a little kid. For all I know, demons come from cabbage patches or get delivered by storks. I know I was turned into one, but I don't know how Ian made it happen. I went to bed with him one night and woke up a demon the next morning. It has to be more complicated than just having sex, though—otherwise, I would have spawned dozens of other demons myself by now, and the whole planet would be populated by demons.

"I don't know."

He gives me an incredulous look.

"Seriously, I don't know. I don't even know how I became a demon."

I look down at my hands. They seem a little darker than usual. I wonder whether it's the lighting or because I just ate a soul. As for sexual characteristics, the only thing I know is that Ian's skin is a deep, dark red while mine is pastel pink. He also has big black horns. My horns are white and really just nubs. I have no way of knowing whether these are gender-related or age-related differences. I'm still not willing to mention Ian to these people, so I keep my questions to myself.

Peter continues to stare at me. "I'm fascinated about the lack of obvious sexual characteristics."

I wish he'd stop talking about it. It's too weird. Now that I think about it, my demon form is rather doll-like: no breasts, no genitalia. I try to picture Ian in demon form. He didn't have any obvious genitals either. Hmm. I wonder what, if anything, that means.

Peter takes something out of his pocket and holds it up. "Do you mind?"

It's a tape measure, the fabric type that tailors use.

"Go ahead."

He measures everything from my horn nubs to the claws on my feet and everything in between. He makes notes in his little notebook. When he's finished, he steps back and looks at me again.

"Could you revert back to human, please?"

"Sure." Just to mess with him, I'm Alma again, naked and as sexy as I can be without changing form.

His cheeks flush pink, and he averts his eyes. "Alma, please."

"Please what?"

"Please put your clothes back on."

What a weird guy. "Why don't you wear a hazmat suit when you deal with me?" I ask as I pull on my clothes.

He clears his throat. "It's not necessary."

"Why not?"

He shifts uneasily. "It just isn't."

"I'm dressed," I say, and he looks at me again. "So, is that how this is going to work?"

"What?"

"You guys get to ask me whatever you want—test me, measure me—but I don't get any answers."

He frowns and paces back and forth. "It's not my place to give you answers, Alma."

"Your place? What are you, a servant? Who do you serve? Sefu?"

He shakes his head, but his cheeks are pink again. "Sefu and I work for the same organization."

"What organization would that be? It's not the church, is it? Because Sefu doesn't strike me as all that religious." I'm so sick of not knowing anything.

He does that little smile thing. "That's a discussion for another time. That's it for today." The goons come into the room, but I don't know how he called for them.

"Escort her back to her room, please."

Chapter 18: A Little Variety

And here I am. Pacing in my little white box. I tried reading, but I'm too agitated. It's clear that Peter knows more than he's telling. He seems to have a different motive than Sefu, not that I really know what Sefu's motive is, mind you. I need to sort this out. I'd like to know whether they work for a larger organization or if this is it. It's one thing to get out of this place. It's quite another to get away from these people if they're part of some international cabal or something. I really want to know how they found me in the first place. How did they know I was a demon? That eats at me. Somehow, it all comes down to quantum mechanics. Physics. Fine, let's start there. I go into the bathroom and stand in front of the mirror. I look as carefully as I can to see if there are any telltale signs as to my true nature, but I don't see any. I wish I knew more about quantum physics, but high school physics just brushes by the subject. The real physics in high school is Newtonian. I've read a couple of magazine articles and saw a documentary once on quantum mechanics but nothing to indicate how you could use it to determine if someone is a demon. This is making me crazy. I used to think my old life sucked, then Ian turned me into a demon and that really sucked, but at least I had freedom of movement. I wasn't trapped like a rat in a cage.

The door opens, and Sefu comes in.

"Peter said you were agitated. What's the problem?"

This guy is unbelievable. "You brought me the *Baltimore Sun*. Please. Can I at least get the *Washington Post*?"

He chuckles, which pisses me off.

"Who do you work for?" I growl.

"For whom," he corrects.

"So you work for grammar Nazis?"

He chuckles again. I'd like to punch him in the teeth and then give him a little kiss.

"I work for an organization called SEU."

"SEU? What does that mean?" I'm a little surprised that he's told me the name.

"It's stands for Seeking the Elegant Universe."

"Weird name for a demon prison."

He smiles at me. "It's a think tank. I run one of its labs."

"And Peter?"

"Is a better scientist than you might imagine."

His straightforward answers take me off guard.

"Why don't you two wear hazmat suits around me?"

"We each have our own methods of resisting your charms."

"And what would those be?"

He shakes his head. "Please, Alma. Only an idiot would answer that question."

Yeah, too bad he's not an idiot.

He raises his eyebrows at me. "Any other questions?"

I frown at him. "Not at the moment."

"Good. Here is your next meal. The guards will escort you up in the morning. This time, I don't want you to call the code. Just get in, collect the sharps, take his soul, and leave." He walks over to the chest of drawers and pulls out one of the badges and hands it to me. "You'll be her this time."

I look at the badge. Christine Jackson, African American, five foot seven, maybe one hundred seventy-five pounds. The badge identifies her as working for a medical waste contractor. Fun.

"Any problems?" Sefu asks.

I turn my face into Christine Jackson's by way of a reply.

He smiles. "You're very good at that."

It annoys me that I'm flattered.

"I'll see you tomorrow, Alma." He heads for the door. Just before he walks out, he adds, "And I'll see what I can do about getting you a copy of the *Post*."

"Thanks," I say before I can stop myself. I just thanked my jailor. I think I'm coming down with Stockholm syndrome. I wonder if there's a cure for that.

When Sefu leaves, I resume pacing. Back and forth, back and forth I go in this tiny white room. I'd climb the walls if I could get purchase. In desperation, I knock on the door. One of the goons opens it.

"Hey," I say. "You guys want to play cards or something?"

Big Gun Guy chuckles.

The other guy shakes his head. "I don't think so."

I knew it was a long shot. "Maybe some other time, then."

I go back into my room and throw myself across the bed and stare at the ceiling until I fall asleep. Yep, another exciting evening.

In the morning, I wake to the sound of a goon knocking on the door. I turn myself into Christine Jackson and get dressed similarly to how I was dressed the last time. The clothes they gave me don't vary much. Nondescript is the style du jour. The hazmat guys escort me to the elevator, and I suck out the soul of a Korean man who appears to be nine hundred years old. As I wheel my cart through the lobby, I can't take it anymore. I leave the cart and walk outside, squinting in the bright sunshine. I'm out there less than a minute before Peter appears.

"You need to go back inside now, Alma."

I sigh. "I just killed a really old guy. Can you give me a minute?" The old man's soul is full and warm in my belly. On top of Oscar's equally satisfying soul, I feel strong, bold.

Peter considers my request. "One more minute."

I close my eyes and soak up all the sunshine I can. I wish I could take some with me back to that white hole I live in now. When I open my eyes again, I realize there are ten people just lingering near us. They're all dressed in regular street clothes, but they're all men, and they're all buff. Some of them are wearing long trench coats that could easily conceal big guns. I'm not getting out of here.

"Okay," I say and walk back to retrieve my cart from the lobby before I return to the elevators. At least now I know that they're always watching me. Sure, I had suspected that, but it's good to know specifics. I have a detail of ten men ready to pounce on me if I get out of line. Great.

We return to the elevators and play the secret wall game, but instead of being escorted back to my room, I'm returned to Peter's lab. I wonder if he's actually a priest. What would a real priest be doing down here? And hey, I'm not even Catholic, so I decide to mess with him a bit.

"So, Pete, what fun games are we going to play today?"

He pauses a moment after I call him Pete, but unfortunately, it doesn't seem to ruffle his feathers too much. Damn, I was hoping for a more amusing reaction. I am seriously bored. Would it kill them to give me a television? Hell, how about a radio, a video game, something?

"I'm going have you run for me today, Alma," old Pete says.

Joy.

He shows me the biggest treadmill I've ever seen. "Does the whole department like to run at the same time?" I ask.

"It's designed for horses. You're a bit heavy for a regular treadmill."

I frown at him. "You were never any good with the ladies, were you?"

He smiles. "No. Step on, please."

I step on, and he starts up the giant treadmill, slowly bringing up the speed until I'm running as fast as I can. He's making notes the whole time. Then he starts backing down the speed until it stops.

"Good," he announces. "Now switch to your demon form, and let's try it again."

A curtain is set up for me to change behind. I'm curious to see just how fast I can run as a demon.

As it turns out, I can run a lot faster in demon form. I knew that, of course, but I didn't realize how much faster. I was doing about ten miles an hour in human form, which I have to say is pretty good, but in demon form, I'm doing closer to thirty. Of course, in demon form, I'm also running on all fours, which is faster. Peter seems duly impressed as he slows the treadmill back to a stop.

"Excellent, Alma. As you can see, you're considerably faster in demon form."

"Yay." Whatever.

"I don't suppose you've ever raced another demon, have you?"

"What other demon?" I ask. As far as I'm willing to say to these people, there are no other demons, just Sugar Pie and me, and they've already killed one of us.

He gives me the little smile again but doesn't push it. "I'd also like to get tissue and blood samples today," he says. "Could you switch back to human form?"

All this switching is annoying because it requires a lot of undressing and redressing. I go back to being Alma, and he asks me to sit down.

I take a seat in a big gray chair. The chair, like the treadmill, is oversize.

"Is this for horses too?" I ask.

He laughs and comes at me with a needle.

I'm not squeamish about having my blood drawn, but I don't love it either. He ties a rubber tourniquet around my arm and tells me to make a fist. He spends a lot of time tapping the bend in my arm and making faces.

"I can't seem to find a vein," he says.

He ponders that for a moment. I probably wouldn't enlighten him, even if I understood why he couldn't find a vein, but I don't. No one has tried to take blood from me since I became a succubus. Then again, I haven't been sick since then either. Curious.

"Okay, switch back to demon form. It makes sense that I can't find a vein if you're masking your true shape somehow."

"Really?" I ask him. "That makes sense to you?"

He actually sighs. "As much as any of this makes sense. I don't know what the mechanism is for you to change your shape, so I really don't know how any of this works."

I shrug. "Fair enough." I step behind the curtain and become Cupcake again.

Only, Peter can't find a vein on Cupcake either. I don't know why, but this amuses me. I can tell he's irritated because his jaw keeps clenching and unclenching.

"Okay, I'll talk to Sefu about the blood work. Let me just get a skin scraping, and I'll let you go back to your room."

"Oh, goody."

Peter does a scraping, only he doesn't seem too happy with it and tries again. This time, he scrapes harder, but honestly, he's just tickling me. My skin isn't very sensitive to pain anymore. After doing the scraping six times, each time bearing down harder and harder, he gives up and calls the guards to return me to my room.

I turn back into Alma and get dressed and give Peter a little wave as I walk out. I get the feeling I messed up his whole day, which is pretty satisfying.

As the guards walk me back to my room, I say, "Hey, you guys up for a card game today?"

The guy with the big gun chuckles.

The other guy says, "I don't think so."

Back in my room, I read both *Time* magazines cover to cover, and then I start on the novel. Days are endless here. A full soul stomach just makes it worse. I have all this energy and nowhere to put it. Running on the treadmill actually helped a bit. I wonder if I should ask to do that every day.

Just as I'm about to see if I can literally bounce off the walls, there's a knock on the door. It's one of the hazmat guys. I can't see their faces, and I can't smell them through their suits, so I can't distinguish one from the other.

He holds up a deck of cards. "We've been given permission to play cards with you."

"Seriously?" I can't believe how excited I am about the prospect of a simple card game.

"Yes, but we have to play in the hallway, and there will be an armed guard in position." His voice comes through a mechanical filter, but it sounds sweet to me.

"Great, I'm in."

I step out into the hall to find not one but two armed guards. The first hazmat guy sits on the floor, and I sit opposite him.

"Since there's just two of us, what do you say to gin rummy?"

"Sounds good," I say.

I used to play rummy with my father, but I'm not interested in mentioning my family to these people. I would prefer for them to think I was spawned somewhere from a pile of ooze.

We play cards for over an hour. No one says anything, but it's nice just to have the company. I win more than I lose but not by a lot. I'm disappointed when hazmat guy says it's the last game.

"I hope we can play again sometime."

"Sure," he says. "I'll see what I can do."

Going back into my room is hard but not as hard as it would have been if I'd just been stuck in there alone all day. I decide to finish reading the novel.

It's after midnight when Sefu comes in again. He's got a large manila envelope in his hand.

"You've been doing very well, Alma," he says.

I don't respond.

"Aside from your unscheduled exit from the building, I think things have been going smoothly."

"You said I could see my mother."

"Yes."

"When?"

"Soon, Alma. It's only been a few days. Trust takes time to build. You must have patience."

I feel like I've been trapped in here for months.

"It seems you've caused Father Peter a great deal of trouble."

"I didn't do anything to him."

He smiles. "Not that sort of trouble. He tells me he couldn't draw blood from you or get a skin scraping in either your succubus state or your human form. Why do you think that is?"

I shrug. "I wouldn't know."

"You haven't been to the doctor since becoming a demon?"

"I haven't been sick."

"Interesting." He walks over to the dresser and picks up the magazines. "Are you done with these?"

"Yeah."

"Tomorrow, Peter is going to attempt to X-ray you. He might even do an MRI. What do you think he'll find going on inside you?"

I shrug again.

Sefu smiles at me, but it's not a nice smile. "I would ask that if you're deliberately making scientific inquiry difficult, that you stop. It won't help your situation if we can't analyze you."

"I'm not doing anything."

He stares at me in that penetrating way he has. Who needs an X-ray? I feel like he can see right through me.

"I believe you. In the interim, if you can think of anything that would make this easier on Peter, I would appreciate it."

Oh sure, I live to make Ol' Pete's life easier. "Okay, can I get some dinner?"

"Ah, yes." Sefu says. "I meant to ask you this before. How many regular meals would you like a day?"

"Three is a nice number."

"Oh," Sefu says, raising his eyebrows. "So many."

"Don't you eat three meals a day?" I ask.

"Yes, but I'm human."

Bully for you, buddy. "Well, I still like to eat."

"Your preference is still chicken soup?"

Mostly, I ate chicken soup to ease the pain of not having enough souls. Now that I'm well fed, I'm willing to mix it up just for something different to do.

"I still like it, but some variety might be nice."

"All right, then." Sefu opens the envelope and hands me a folded newspaper, two *Entertainment Weekly*s, and another book. He takes the others from the top of my chest of drawers. "Have a good night, Alma."

I don't wish him the same as he leaves.

Chapter 19: Solid State

The next morning after a breakfast of eggs and toast, I'm escorted back to Peter's lab. He's clearly excited about today's experiments. I'm less excited.

"Okay, Alma, if you'll just lie down over here."

I lie on a big table. I recognize it as an X-ray table from when I broke my arm as a kid, although this table is a lot bigger than that one was. Peter steps behind a partition, and a large mechanical arm starts moving over me. He takes a lot of X-rays. I wonder if that's safe. I don't know how X-rays affect me now. For all I know, he could be killing me. After a while, the big arm stops moving, but Peter doesn't hurry back out to me. I can hear him muttering to himself, but I can't understand what he's saying.

"Can I get up now?" I ask.

"Not just yet, Alma. Can you transform?"

Bored, I comply. He does the whole process over again. The muttering continues. Eventually, the machine powers down.

He steps out from behind the partition with his cell phone to his ear. "If you could just come down, I'm asking for five minutes," he says to whoever he's talking to.

I continue lying on the table.

"You can transform back if you want," he says.

I do and get dressed.

A few minutes later, Sefu comes in. He nods at me and then follows Peter behind the partition. I can hear Sefu laughing.

"It's not funny!" Peter says as they walk over to me.

Sefu clicks on a monitor that's mounted to the wall. He brings up several X-rays on the screen. "These are yours," he says to me.

They just look like white blurs. I lean in for a closer look. It doesn't help. They still look like white blurs. "Where are my bones?"

"Where indeed!" Sefu says, clearly delighted. "Have you tried an MRI yet?"

Peter shakes his head. I notice for the first time that he's not wearing his white collar. He's still in a black suit but without the collar. I wonder why.

"Do the MRI," Sefu says. "Call me when you're done. I have to go. I have an appointment."

I wonder what kind of appointment it is. Does Sefu see regular patients, or does he have other creatures like me to see? He sweeps out of the room like a king, like he's wearing an imaginary cape or something.

"Bossy guy," I say to Peter.

He shrugs. "Come over here. Let's do the MRI."

He directs me to lie down in a large tube, bigger than the one they put my mother in when she hurt her knee. I'm guessing it's also for veterinary use. MRIs are not that fun. I have to lie perfectly still, and then it sounds like a group of lunatics sits on top of the tube and beats it with a hammer. It's very headache inducing. I'm in there for twenty minutes, which is twenty minutes too long. When Peter finally pulls me out, he's clearly confused.

"What?"

He pushes his fingers back through his hair. "I don't understand."

"What?" I repeat.

"The images are all uniform, as if you're one solid piece inside."

"Seriously?" That's weird. "Maybe you're having an equipment malfunction."

He frowns. "Maybe."

"Hey, can I run on the treadmill again? It keeps me from being so antsy in my room."

"Sure," he says, distracted.

I get on the treadmill and set it for a reasonable pace. Peter starts fooling with the MRI equipment and seems to forget about me. This would be a wonderful opportunity to get the hell out of here if it weren't for all the guards.

When I'm done on the treadmill, he's still futzing with the equipment. I'm not used to being ignored, I guess, because against my better judgment, I walk over to him. "How's it going?"

"I can't find anything wrong." He types something on the keyboard. A diagnostic starts on the screen.

"Why aren't you wearing your collar?"

He looks up from the keyboard. "What do you care? You're not Catholic."

"Don't you care?"

He sighs. "I don't really practice anymore. It seemed disingenuous to keep wearing it."

"So you're not a priest anymore?"

Peter laughs, but it's a dry, brittle sound. "Once a priest, always a priest, whether you practice or not."

"Seriously? Being a priest sounds like going to prison."

He looks at me like I'm crazy.

"You know, because even when you're out, it follows you everywhere."

He frowns at me. He seems so down I almost feel bad for the guy. I wonder, not for the first time, how he ended up here. No harm in asking, I guess.

"Why are you here, instead of in some nice little parish somewhere, listening to confessions and passing the collection plate?"

This time, when he looks at me, he's teary-eyed. "I have no idea. Guards!"

The sudden change surprises me, and the hazmat guys take me back to my room. Sadly, there is no card game in the hall this time. I spend the next few hours reading and trying to figure out what's going on with Peter.

I haven't arrived at any stunning conclusions when Sefu comes in with another manila folder in his hands. "Good afternoon, Alma," he says.

"Hi."

He takes a deep breath and lets it out slowly as he walks around my room. "Have you considered what you're going to tell your mother to explain your absence?"

Alarm bells go off in my head. I don't like him talking about my mother, but the possibility of seeing her again is exciting. "Not really."

"You need to decide," he says firmly in that irritating way of his. "You'll be seeing her tomorrow, if all goes well."

My heart sings to the sound of that, but I'm not stupid. "If all what goes well?"

"I have a mission for you. It's local, straightforward, and you'll have backup."

Translation: I'll be watched. "What mission?"

He opens the folder and shows me the picture of a thug. The guy has a scar on his cheek, a spiderweb tattoo on his neck, and a snarl on his face.

"This gentleman just got off on six counts of rape and two counts of homicide on a technicality. With luck like that, I think he deserves a kiss, don't you?"

Now I think I understand why Peter was so upset. There is no way this is covered under some research grant.

"This guy hurt someone you know?"

"Let's say yes."

That's a weird reply. I wonder what it means. "How am I supposed to find him?"

"He frequents a bar in your old feeding grounds. The guards will take you there. When you've completed your task, you'll be taken to your mother's house for a visit."

"Okay, so when is this happening?"

He looks at the clock. "You'll be leaving in a few minutes."

"Well, thanks for the notification. Nothing like last-minute planning."

"You have everything you need. It's not like you have to get gear together."

"Nope. I've got lips, so I'm good."

"Exactly. I'll see you when you return."

Ten minutes later, I'm in the back of a white van cruising down 695. There is a thick plexiglass divider between the guys up front and me. They aren't wearing hazmat suits, and I can tell from their voices that one of them is the guy who played cards with me. I consider my options. I know I can get through the plexiglass. I can also get through the doors at the back of the van, locked or not. I have a serious choice here. This is the perfect opportunity to escape. But then what? Does Sefu track me down and kill me? Do I go back to working for Ian? I consider Ian and Sefu. They're both controlling assholes. At least when I worked for Ian, I had my freedom, but I was always scrounging for souls, which I then had to share. Sefu provides me with a steady supply of souls, and I don't have to track guys anymore. On the other hand, killing is killing, and Sefu keeps me captive. Maybe if I pull off this job for him, if I get him to trust me, maybe that will change. It's a risk either way.

I open the folder Sefu gave me. In addition to a picture of the thug, there are pictures of the women he raped, two of whom he murdered. He has a thing for petite redheads. Lucky him, I have a thing for assholes. I go back and forth over whether to do the job or escape all the way to Virginia. When we finally arrive at Dave's Bar & Grille on Route

1, I've made up my mind. I step out of the van looking like one of his victims. One of the guards actually tells me to be careful. Isn't that cute?

Dave's Bar & Grille is—and I want to put this in the politest possible terms—a shithole. It's the kind of place no decent man or woman should ever walk into. If I were still human, I wouldn't go within a hundred yards of this place. The sign above the door is blinking off and on like a warning. The whole place practically screams "attack me." Perfect.

I'm wearing one of my outfits from the hospital. When I walk in, I go straight to the bar. "You got a phone I can use?" I ask. "My car broke down, and my cell is dead."

I can see the thug perk up. He's sitting at the other end of the bar. There aren't ten customers in the whole joint.

"There's a pay phone by the bathrooms, but it ain't working."

The thug appears by my side. "You can use my phone, lady."

He hands me a prepaid cell. This guy is no dummy. He doesn't want the police to be able to track his calls.

I call my father's old work number knowing no one is there after five o'clock. When it goes to voice mail, I click the phone off.

"My boyfriend isn't answering," I tell the thug.

"What's wrong with your car?" he asks. "Maybe I can help. I'm good with cars."

The bartender is pulling another beer for a guy who looks like he's already had too many.

"That would be great," I tell the thug. "It just stopped working. I pulled over on a side street not far from here. This is the first place I came to."

He nods and follows me out. "Sounds like it may be the alternator. I might be able to rig something up for you."

I take the first side street I come to. The guy sounds so sincere. I can see how he might have tricked those other women. I'm a little different, though. I can hear his heartbeat increase with the lie, and I can smell the pheromones coming off of him in waves. The minute we turn off the main road and into the darkened side street, he comes at me. He punches me so hard in the back of the head that if I were human, it probably would have knocked me out. But I'm not human. As it is, I don't even stumble. I turn around and grab the front of his shirt. This is an unexpected turn of events for him. He doesn't even react right away, which is his downfall. I've got my mouth over his before he even knows what's happening, and I'm sucking like my life depends on it, and let's face it, in some ways, it does. It's not a very pleasant experience. His mouth tastes like an ashtray soaked in beer. Not surprisingly, he has a meager soul. It hardly constitutes a meal, but I ate yesterday. I let go of him, and he falls backward, his head making a very satisfying thud as it hits the sidewalk. I can see the white van turning onto the side street. Happy to be seeing my mother soon, I start toward the van.

"Going somewhere, Cupcake?" Ian's voice stops me cold.

I can smell him. He's behind me, and the van is still coming toward me.

"You wouldn't be thinking of leaving, now, would you?" Ian growls. "You owe me. Where have you been, Cupcake?"

I turn to face him. "I was just coming to see you, Ian."

He laughs and steps from the shadows. He's in his nasty pimp form. I hate this form. It makes him exceptionally mean. I hear the van stop behind me. I wonder if Ian has made the connection between the van and me.

"Why don't I believe you?" Ian asks.

"Leave, Ian," I whisper. "Leave right now."

He narrows his eyes at me.

I can hear the chirp of a radio behind me, and one of the guards says, "We have a situation."

Ian hears it too. "What is this?" he growls.

A distinct sound whines through the night. It's the big gun charging. I remember that sound from the night they caught me.

"Run!" I say under my breath.

Instead, Ian drops his disguise and goes into full incubus mode. He's larger than I've ever seen him. I step back.

He roars into the night and goes running at the van, head down, horns forward. He hits the van like a charging ram and knocks it across the street. The guy with the gun fires, but he misses. Ian is shockingly fast for such a big creature. I realize the gun won't recharge in time for them to get a second shot in before he can reach them. I'm not sure what he'll do if he can get his hands on them, but I'm sure it won't be pretty. I drop my human façade and go full succubus mode. I can't stop Ian. He's stronger than I am, but I can slow him down. I can tell from the look on the guys' faces that they don't know what me in monster mode means.

I pick up an old Harley that's parked on the side of the road and throw it at Ian's head as hard as I can.

"Traitor!" he growls at me. "I made you."

"Yeah," I growl back. "That's why I threw the Harley at you."

The whine of the gun charging starts again. Ian looks from me to the guards. He can take one or the other but not both. He cuts his losses and charges into the night at top speed.

The guys look at me askance, but they don't raise the gun in my direction.

To allay their fears, I transform back into my original human form, the one they're used to seeing. Unfortunately, this leaves me naked since I blew apart my clothes when I went into monster mode.

Their mouths drop open, but they also look really relieved. One of the guys gets a tarp out of the back of the van, and I wrap it around myself. I wonder if this will affect getting to see my mother. There is a huge dent on the side of the van where Ian rammed it. The driver's-side door won't open, so the guard with the gun gets into the back of the van with me. He doesn't have a hazmat suit.

"We're going to have to go back to the center and debrief Sefu on the attack," the driver tells me.

"Are you okay?" Gun Guard asks.

"Yeah, I'm fine," I tell him. "Just a little cold." But it's not the temperature that's bothering me.

"Turn up the heat, John," he tells the driver.

John does, and pretty soon, it warms up, but I still feel cold inside. The rest of the drive to Baltimore passes in silence. The guards still seem a little freaked out, and I'm pretty freaked out myself. Tonight, I made a critical decision. I chose sides. Clearly, Ian was disgusted by my choice. Maybe I should be too. Have I turned my back on my own kind? Maybe, but I want to be human again. Besides, I just couldn't let him kill those guys. And yes, I recognize the irony in that. Maybe I have Stockholm syndrome. I don't owe Ian anything but trouble. He put me in this situation. He's just going to have to cope with how I'm handling it.

Sefu and two guards are waiting for us as the van pulls into the parking garage.

"I'll come and see you in a little while," Sefu tells me. "Go and get dressed."

The two guards that are standing with Sefu escort me back to my room. I'm surprised to find Peter waiting there.

He looks surprised to see me. "Hello," he says. "What's with the tarp?"

"I ran into a little trouble," I tell him.

It surprises me that he doesn't know this already. I wonder if he's faking not knowing. Peter looks weird. He's out of his collar again, but now he's in a tight black T-shirt and jeans. I've never seen him look so casual. I'm really too tired to worry about it right now, though. I go sit next to him on the bed, hoping he'll take the hint and go away. He doesn't.

"What do you miss most about being human?" he asks out of the blue.

I think about that. "Being touched," I answer honestly. "I can't remember the last time someone hugged me."

He gives me an odd look, and then he hugs me. The tarp makes a crinkling sound as he does so. It's very weird to be sitting on my bed wearing nothing but a blue plastic sheet, being hugged by a priest who seems to have forgotten he's a priest. The hug is awkward but oddly comforting, even though he's careful not to let any of his skin touch mine. After a moment, he lets me go and stands to leave.

And then it dawns on me. Suddenly, I realize why he's on this project, why he's stopped wearing his collar, why Sefu's plans are of such concern to him.

"How long have you been in love with him?" I ask.

His shoulders tense up. He stops but doesn't turn around. "Good night, Alma."

"Does Sefu know how you feel? Is he even gay?"

Peter still doesn't look at me, but he shrugs before stepping into the hallway and closing the door behind him.

Even though he didn't really say so, I'm sure Peter is in love with Sefu. This is too much information but not nearly enough. I wonder if Sefu knows and what that might mean. I shower and brush my teeth and put on a T-shirt and some yoga pants. I don't put on any underwear. I don't need it. Most of the time, I just look like a Barbie doll under my clothes. It's too much effort to look completely human all the time, so lately, I only bother with the parts that show.

Chapter 20: Two Truths and a Lie

As expected, Sefu shows up a few minutes later and hands me a couple of paperback mysteries.

"Thanks."

He nods and begins pacing. "That creature that attacked the van, do you know it?"

So here it is. How far do I go? I weigh my options. I did throw a motorcycle at Ian's head. In for a penny, in for a pound, I guess.

"Yes. He's an incubus."

Sefu turns sharply and stares at me. "He was much larger than you. Is that a gender distinction?"

I shrug.

"Come on, Alma!" he shouts.

"What? I don't know. It could be."

He lets out a frustrated sigh. "Well, what about the other incubi you've met—are they larger than you?"

I shrug again.

"Now you're stonewalling."

"I'm not. I've never seen another incubus in natural form, so I don't know."

"But you have seen other incubi?"

"A few."

"If they were in human form, how did you know they were incubi?"

"They reeked of demon."

He narrows his eyes. "Demons have a particular odor? I've never noticed a smell about you."

I shrug again.

"Stop doing that!"

"Okay, okay. I don't think humans can smell it. Demons don't like to be around each other because of the stench."

"Well, that explains a lot," Sefu says as he starts pacing again.

"Like what?"

He waves a hand at me and keeps pacing.

I don't like being blown off. "Have you seen Peter lately?" I ask.

That makes him pay attention. "Why?"

I start to shrug but stop myself. "He's acting kind of weird lately. He's stopped wearing his collar. Tonight, he was in a really tight T-shirt. Kind of a sexy look for a priest, don't you think?"

Sefu frowns at me. "Tonight? You saw him tonight?"

"He was waiting for me when I got back."

"He didn't have a meeting scheduled with you."

I smile at him. "It must have been impromptu."

His frown deepens, and a line forms between his eyebrows. "I'll talk to you later, Alma."

"Hey," I say as his hand touches the door. "Do I still get to see my mom?"

Sefu turns to look at me. "You completed your mission, so I'll keep my end of the bargain, but you must be patient. We need to sort out how to cope with your friend if he shows up again."

"He's not my friend."

"Well, whoever he is, his presence is problematic to say the least, but I'll do what I can so you can see your mother."

Then he's gone. I wonder what he's going to say to Peter. I'm curious but not curious enough to stay up worrying about it, so I go to bed, taking one of the new books with me.

A knock on the door wakes me from a sound sleep. Oddly, no one walks in after the knock. Bleary-eyed, I open the door. Two guards are standing outside waiting for me.

"We were told to take you to see your mother," the gun guard says.

Gun Guard was the one who asked the driver to turn up the heat last night. I like him. He almost treats me like a person.

"Yes," I answer, "I'll be ready in a jiff."

I shower and dress in record time. I'm so excited to see my mother but a little worried too. I've been gone a long time without contacting her. I feel really bad about what she must've been going through.

As we're walking to the van, the guards tell me the rules. I only get an hour. I can't leave the house beyond the yard. Just as we're getting ready to leave, Sefu shows up and hands me a piece of paper.

"You can give this number to your mother," he says.

I look at the phone number.

"Otherwise, I don't care what you tell her to explain your absence as long as it isn't the truth."

I nod my response. He looks off today. There are bags under his eyes, and he doesn't seem his usual confident self. I'd ask him about it if I cared.

The drive to my mom's house takes over an hour. I listen to the radio and work on my cover story to pass the time. Like all lies, it should be as simple and as close to the truth as possible. That makes it easier to remember and easier to maintain.

When we finally arrive, it's all I can do not to tear off the van doors. I take deep breaths while the guards let me out.

I'm disappointed to find that no one answers the door when I ring the bell.

All the excitement drains out of me in a rush. I'm not going to get to see her. Who knows when or even if I'll have this chance again?

Despondent, I walk back to the van. "Are you sure she's here?" I ask the guards.

"Intel says she's here," they assure me.

I walk around to the backyard. She's sweeping the deck.

"Mama?"

She turns around, and the broom drops from her hands, clattering against the decking. "Alma," she cries as she runs toward me.

I've never been so happy to be hugged in my life. It's such an intense relief to see her again that I start crying too. Unfortunately, my tears are acid, so I quickly back away from her and wipe my face.

"Oh, Alma," Mom says. "Where have you been? I've been worried sick."

"I'm sorry, Mom, but it was part of the treatment." I've always been a good liar. This is no exception.

"Treatment?" Mom asks.

"Let's go in, maybe have a cup of tea."

"Of course," she says and pushes back the sliding glass door that leads into the eat-in kitchen area.

"I only have an hour," I tell her.

"So short?" she says. She gives me that wounded look that I hate so much. She used to give that look to my dad a lot.

"It's one of the program rules," I tell her, which isn't really a lie, assuming you're comfortable with referring to the organization that captured me as a "program."

"What program?" Mom asks as she plugs in the electric kettle.

"I'm finally getting clean, Mom."

"Oh, Alma!" she says and rushes over to hug me again.

"It's okay, Mom. It's a strict program, but it's a good one."

She sits down at the table. "But, Alma, how are you paying for it?"

"It's a federally funded trial program up in Maryland. I'm lucky to have been selected." Selected, kidnapped, what's the difference?

She nods at me, completely convinced of the luck of my selection, but then that's my mother. She never met a lie she wasn't willing to believe if it painted her loved ones in a better light.

"How did you find the program?" she asks, eager for details.

"I didn't really. They found me. I met this priest, and he suggested I join."

"A priest? Does he know you're not Catholic?" Her forehead wrinkles with concern.

She's afraid I've lied my way into drug rehab. She might like it when I'm painted in a better light, but she doesn't have high expectations.

"I told you it's federally funded. The priest just works there. It's not Catholic Charities."

"They let them do that?"

I shrug. "I don't know what they let priests do. I'm not Catholic."

I smile at her, and she smiles back.

The kettle clicks off, and she gets up to make the tea. "I do wish you'd called," she says while her back is still to me.

This is as confrontational as my mother gets.

"I would have," I say, "but the program didn't allow it."

Once again, not really a lie. This lie is telling itself.

"That's terrible," she says, bringing the tea to the table.

I put a spoonful of sugar in mine while Mom gets a little pitcher of milk.

"Not really," I tell her. "I had to earn the right to be with my family by being clean. I really wanted to see you, so I worked really hard."

This brings her to tears. She wipes her eyes while I put a little milk in my tea. I slide the piece of paper Sefu gave me across the table to her.

"You can call me at this number."

I sip my tea as she looks at the number.

"This is to the center?" she asks.

"Yeah, if you call, someone will come get me."

She nods. "How long will you have to be there?"

Ooh, tough question. "Uh, I don't know. I guess until I can face life without drugs."

She gives me the sad face again. "I was so hoping you were going to be able to avoid drugs, Alma. After everything your father went through, I didn't want that life for you."

I cover her hand with mine. "I know. I'm sorry I disappointed you, but I'm going to pull myself together. You'll see."

She pats my hand on top of hers. "I know you will, Alma. I know you will."

This is getting a little too heavy for me. I don't want to cry and ruin the finish on the table. Plus, you know, acid tears are hard to explain.

"Well, enough about that," I say, giving her a big smile. "What have you been up to while I've been gone?"

"Well," she starts.

We walk through the house and the yard, looking at all the little projects my mother has been working on. She wants to get flower boxes for the deck, but they didn't have the color she wanted at Target. She's been making fleece lap blankets for the injured soldiers at the VA. She's been pulling a lot of overtime at work but expects that to lighten up pretty soon. It's all very normal. I realize that my mother has always been very good at keeping herself busy no matter what kind of crisis has been going on with the family. It's very productive coping.

I check my watch and realize I need to head back to the van. I don't want them to come looking for me. "Look, Mama, I've got to go."

"Okay, sweetie," she says.

We walk back to the front door, and I kiss her cheek.

"I'll be back."

"When?"

"I'm not sure, but I'll try to make it soon, okay?"

She squeezes my forearm. "Okay."

We hug, and I head for the van.

The drive back has me thinking. While it's not ideal, my current situation is, in many ways, better than being with Ian. On the other hand, while I don't particularly mind working for Sefu, I don't want to be held prisoner. I wonder if there's a way to win his trust enough to let me live on my own. In strictly practical terms, I'm better off now. I have a steady supply of souls, and I don't have to share them with anyone. I just don't want to be locked up. I want out. Although if I'm out, I have to deal with Ian, and I'm not sure how to do that.

Sefu is waiting for us when we pull into the garage.

"Come with me, Alma," he says, and I follow him to his office.

He offers me a seat, and I sit in one of the leather chairs in front of his desk. He takes his seat behind his desk and steeples his fingers.

"How did the visit with your mother go?"

"Fine."

I'm disinclined to talk too much about her. Sefu is the kind of guy who files every little thing he hears away for use later. He's got enough on me that he can use. There's no reason to add anything.

He doesn't say anything for a moment, waiting to see if I'll elaborate. When I don't, he asks, "What excuse did you give her for your absence?"

"I told her I was in rehab."

He gives me a penetrating look. "You have a history with drugs?"

"No, but it was a convenient way to explain the demon stuff."

He purses his lips in thought. "That's quite clever."

"Try not to sound so surprised."

He chuckles.

It's all very chummy. Or at least, it would be if he weren't holding me captive.

"How did you feel about your assignment?"

"What do you mean?"

"Did you enjoy it?"

I think about that for a moment. With the exception of Ian showing up, I did enjoy it. I hadn't considered that before. I'd mostly focused on the part where Ian appeared. I'm a little disturbed to realize how satisfying tricking that guy and taking his soul was. I'd like to say it was because he was scumbag rapist, and that's certainly part of it, but to be honest, it's not all of it. That makes me feel a little less human and a little more demon than is really comfortable.

"It was okay," I say to Sefu.

He gives me another one of those penetrating looks, and I sense he knows I'm playing it down.

"Then you wouldn't be opposed to another similar mission."

I shrug, intentionally because I know it irritates him.

He huffs at me.

"I guess not," I say, "but what about Ian?"

He drums his fingers on his desk. "What indeed?"

We sit in silence for a moment.

"Let me think about it," he finally says. He taps the intercom on his desk and asks for the guards to come and escort me back to my room.

"You ever going to let me just walk there on my own?" I ask.

He looks at me, sizing me up. "Perhaps one day, Alma."

The guards show up, and it's back to the white box for me.

Chapter 21: Road Trip

I spend several boring hours reading in my room until I'm interrupted by a knock on the door, followed by Peter's entrance. I wonder if Sefu knows he's here this time.

"Good evening, Alma," Peter says.

He's back in his black suit and priest's collar. I wonder what that means.

"How are you feeling after your first excursion?"

Excursion? That's an interesting thing to call it unless he's just talking about the visit with my mother.

"I'm good," I say, but now I'm wondering if Peter even knows the real extent of the night's events.

"I'm sure you were excited to be able to see your mother."

"Yeah, it was great. It would be greater if I could see her whenever I wanted."

He smiles. "Yes, well..."

There's an awkward silence as he lets his last statement drop. Well, what? I wonder whether Peter has any input into my situation or if he's just here to observe. He doesn't seem to be Sefu's equal, but I don't know that he technically works for him either. I wish I could see some kind of organizational chart for this place, which just serves as a reminder that this situation is just as strange and confusing as working for Ian was.

He changes the subject. "I've been thinking about why MRIs and X-rays don't work on you."

Right now, I couldn't care less.

"I think you might be multidimensional."

Okay, what? I can't help myself; I have to ask. "What?"

"I have a theory that the reason you can do what you do is that you have more control over the individual molecules, possibly even the particles, of your form. I think you might be shifting particles you don't need into another dimension. The reason the X-ray and the MRI show you as having a uniform interior is that you might be pure energy with just a shell of matter."

What the hell?

"I need to understand the mechanism you use to transform and how you take souls."

I don't say anything. I have no idea how I do those things. I just do them.

"Well," he prompts.

I shrug.

"Alma, don't stonewall."

"I'm not. I don't know how I do that stuff."

He frowns at me. "How can you not know what you're doing?"

I shrug again.

He rolls his eyes and starts to pace. "So from the time you became a demon, you could do those things?"

"Pretty much."

"How did you know what you could and couldn't do?"

"Trial and error."

I keep waiting for him to mention Ian, but he doesn't, which means he doesn't know about last night.

"Are you saying you just woke up hungry one morning, killed some guy, and took his soul?"

"Not exactly."

I don't want to talk about this. The whole experience of becoming a succubus is something I'd rather forget. I went to bed with someone I loved, someone I thought loved me, and I woke up a monster. Ian laughed at me when I screamed. He let me starve for hours before he told me what I needed to do to stop the pain. The first guy I killed was a frat boy. He was drunk and had wandered away from his friends. He was young and healthy and had a nice big soul. I took his soul up against a dumpster behind the student union. I had never felt so full and satisfied in my life as I did when I took that very first soul. I've also never hated myself more. I cried all the way home. This was before my tears became acidic. It was easier to let myself cry then.

"How exactly?" Peter prompts me.

"I'm not sure. I don't remember those first few days very well. It's all very fuzzy."

He frowns at me but seems to accept what I'm saying. "I was hoping, since you're such a young demon, that you might remember the transformation. I need someone who has a full understanding of the mechanism."

I shrug. "Sorry, that's not me."

Then I have a thought. How about the creepy guy from the hotel? Didn't Ian say something about him getting his soul back? Surely, if anyone understands the mechanism behind all this, it would be that guy. I look at Peter, sizing him up. The truth is, I feel bad for the guy. I'm a sucker for that sort of thing. Besides, if I help them, they might give me more freedom.

"I might know a guy who can help you."

He perks up a bit at the sound of that. "Really? Who?"

"I don't know his name, but I can take you to him. He's in Falls Church."

"Virginia?" Peter says it like it's Mars.

"Yes, Virginia. I'm from there. It's not like I'm here by choice, remember?"

He has the decency to look embarrassed.

"I'm willing to take you there, if you want to go."

Peter narrows his eyes at me, and I can tell he doesn't entirely trust me, but he wants to. "I'd have to clear it with Sefu."

"Sure," I say. I try to keep my voice casual, like I don't care if we go or not.

Peter leaves, and I'm back to staring at the walls. I've already read everything they've given me. A song about counting flowers on the wall is on continuous loop in my head. My father used to love the Statler Brothers. Unfortunately, there are no flowers on my wall to count, so I'm stuck staring at the clock and hoping to doze off.

A couple of hours later, Sefu shows up at my door rolling a cart with an old-school fat TV on top and a DVD player on the shelf under it next to a stack of DVDs. It also has a few more paperback mysteries and a newspaper on the bottom shelf. I wish I wasn't as excited as I am, but I can't help myself. It's dead boring in here. A metal cart full of old electronics never looked so good.

"I thought you might like a change of pace," Sefu says.

"So you brought me 1995," I say, trying to keep the joy out of my voice even as I wonder where he unearthed the old setup.

He hands me a slip of paper with a name and room number on it along with my identity for the job. "When you're finished collecting this soul, Peter wants to take you on a little trip to Virginia. He believes you know someone there who can help him with his research."

"I think I do."

Sefu nods then gives me a very serious, penetrating stare. "I think it would be wise, Alma, to leave Peter out of your extracurricular missions."

I raise my eyebrows at him but don't say anything.

"There are some ethical issues there that I think would disturb him. I see no reason to upset him unnecessarily."

"I thought you guys were partners."

"Not exactly. You could say he's more theoretical and I'm more practical."

"Ah," I say. "Well, fine by me."

When he leaves, I transform into Sandra Jones, a slender black woman with a sad face. Not for the first time, I wonder where he gets these photos. I pull some clothes out and get dressed.

The television is on in Tim Jackson's room. I stand there, watching the weather forecast for a moment, and then look out the window. Rain. Great. I hate that it's raining on one of the few days I get to see outside. Oh well, back to the job at hand. Jackson is ninety-eight, and pretty much every system in his body is failing. His soul practically leaps into my mouth. I guess I wouldn't want to be trapped in that body anymore either. I empty the trash from his room into my cleaning cart and stroll down the hall. By the time the nurses have entered his room, I'm already at the elevators.

When I return, Peter is waiting for me with two of the goons with big guns. We all walk out to the van. This is the first time I've seen more than one of the special guns.

"What's with double guns?" I ask Peter. I didn't even know they had two.

"Sefu seemed to think that since the second gun was finished, we should bring it."

They only have two. Good to know. "How much does one of those bad boys cost?" I ask as we pull out of the garage.

"Let's just say the cost is astronomical and leave it at that." He pulls out a laptop and turns it on, a clear indicator that he doesn't want to talk.

I sit back and stare out the windshield. I wish I had a window of my own, but the van doesn't have any windows in the back.

After what seems like forever, Peter closes the lid of his laptop. "So, where did you say you met this man?"

"I didn't, but I met him at the hotel we're going to."

Peter frowns. "What were you doing at a hotel so close to where you live?"

I shrug. "You know, this and that."

His frown deepens. "That's not an answer."

"I live with my mother. Don't make me spell it out for you."

He blushes, which delights me to no end. I know it shouldn't, but I can't help myself. I'm mean that way, and let's face it, I'm mean in a lot worse ways than that.

He clears his throat. "So how did you guys meet?"

"We didn't really meet," I say. "He works at the front desk."

"Then what makes you think he can help me?"

"He's creepy."

"That's it? He's creepy, so he can answer complex metaphysical questions?"

I smile at him. "He also smells funny."

"Smells funny? Alma, please."

"He smells kind of like a demon, kind of like a human. It's creepy."

"Well, I hope you're right. It's a long way to go for someone who smells funny."

He's silent for the rest of the drive, but I chat with the guards up front. When we finally arrive through the nightmare of traffic that is the Baltimore–DC corridor, the guards wait outside in the van while Peter and I go into the hotel. I notice they're trusting me more and more. I like that. It makes me feel less like a prisoner. Baby steps.

Creepy Guy is walking in at the same time we are.

"Hey!" I call.

He turns around and looks at me and then starts backing up.

"Don't freak out, man. I just want to talk to you."

He's backed himself into a car. He starts looking around all panicky.

Peter and I walk toward him. I can hear the big guns charging in the van. Clearly, the guys don't want another Ian situation.

"I got no beef with you, Cupcake!" Creepy Guy says, holding out his hand for me to stop.

"I got no beef with you either," I tell him as soothingly as possible. "My friend here just has some questions, and I think you can answer them."

He shakes his head. "I don't think Ian would like that."

"This isn't about Ian. It's about me. Come on, man. It's no big deal. Ian doesn't even have to know."

"What are you talking about?" Creepy Guy says, his eyes wild. "Ian probably already knows. He's been sniffing around for you for days. You are seriously on his shit list."

I look at Peter. "Change of plans. We're going to need to bring him with us."

He frowns at me but signals the guards. Creepy Guy starts to run, but he doesn't get very far. Inside a minute, he's handcuffed and stuffed in the back of the van.

"I'm sorry to have to do this," Peter says quietly as he puts a blindfold on the guy.

"Where are you taking me?" Creepy Guy asks. He sounds a lot calmer than I expected.

"Someplace safe, where we can talk."

"Listen, Cupcake. Let me go. This is not a good idea." I can smell demon funk rolling off him. Clearly, there's more to Creepy Guy than meets the eye.

One of the guards is in the back of the van with us. I look at him. "I think you better shoot him, or we're going to have a serious problem."

The guard doesn't hesitate, and Creepy Guy slumps over, unconscious. Peter's eyes are huge with shock.

"Trust me," I tell him. "Demon funk was coming off him something fierce. If he transformed in the back of this van on the Beltway, I doubt anyone but him and me would survive."

Peter swallows hard and nods. He calls Sefu on his cell phone, while one of the goons pats down Creepy Guy. They take his keys, his cell phone, his wallet, even the change in his pocket. I'm sitting next to the goon, checking his wallet, and see that Creepy Guy's name is Jerry Field and he lives in Annandale. No one says much on the drive back to Baltimore, and I realize I've made a very serious choice here, even more serious than when I threw the Harley at Ian. There's no coming back from this. I'm in it with these people, and that scares me, because I still don't know what they're doing.

Chapter 22: Jerry

Sefu is there to meet us when we arrive. I can see the fury on his face as we drive up. He starts in as soon as the van door opens.

"What are you doing?" he growls through clenched teeth. "You were supposed to be going to talk to someone. How did this happen?"

Peter's mouth is set in a grim line. "Can we talk privately, please?"

Sefu turns to the guards. "Box him, maximum security."

I start to follow the guards.

"Alma, you're with us," Sefu says.

The shock on Peter's face tells me volumes about who's really in charge.

"She's part of this," Sefu says in answer to Peter's unasked question. "You chose this. You can't back out now."

I don't know how to feel as I follow them down the hall to Sefu's office. The second the office door closes behind us, Sefu says, "Explain."

Peter takes a seat. He seems pale. He opens his mouth to say something but then doesn't.

Sefu seems to be getting angrier by the second.

"It was my call," I say. "It happened really fast. I was afraid…" Sefu had told me not to mention the other night, so I fumble for an explanation. "Of an incident out in the open, so it seemed prudent to bring him with us."

Sefu narrows his eyes at Peter, who holds his hands out in supplication. "What did you want me to do? She said the situation was dangerous, and I believed her."

Sighing, Sefu takes a seat and looks at me again. "What is it exactly that you've brought me, Alma?"

"I'm not sure, but I think you'll find him interesting. He's different."

"Different how? What kind of demon is he?"

I'm not sure what to say, since I don't really know.

"Alma?" Sefu looks at me very intently, like Peter isn't in the room.

"I'm not sure, but it's been implied that he used to be an incubus, but now he has his soul back. He didn't smell exactly like a demon the first time I met him, but he was definitely giving off a weird vibe. Then in the van, when he wanted out and started to get pissed about it, he stank like a demon."

Sefu leans back in his chair and steeples his fingers together. He doesn't say anything for what seems like a long time. Finally, he looks at Peter.

"Go monitor him. Let me know when he wakes up."

Peter glances at me.

"Go now," Sefu insists.

Peter is clearly irritated that I'm staying, but he leaves. When the door closes behind him, Sefu turns back to me.

"What were you afraid of?"

"Ian. Jerry said he probably knew I was at the hotel. You told me not to tell Peter about what happened the other night, so I figured that included allowing him to witness a run-in with Ian."

Sefu nods. "Good choice. Thank you."

"The thing is," I continue. "We're going to have to do something about Ian. He's not going to let it rest. He thinks he owns me."

Sefu raises his eyebrows.

"Yeah, I know," I say, rolling my eyes. "You do too."

"I don't think I own you, Alma."

His voice is smooth and silky. It's very appealing, which irritates me.

"I captured you, yes, but not with the intention of owning you."

"Oh? Then what are your intentions?"

He stands. "I wish to work with you. Can you not see that?"

"Work with me? What's that supposed to mean?"

"What it always means," Sefu says and leaves the room. As he exits, a goon comes in to escort me back to my room.

I spend the next couple of hours trying to suss out what working with Sefu is supposed to entail. I mean, is it just more of the same, or is there a larger goal? Sefu seems like a larger-goal kind of guy, so I'm sure I haven't seen the extent of the "work" I'll be doing.

There's a knock at the door, and one of the hazmat goons asks me to come with him. I follow him down the hall toward the holding area where they had me when I first arrived. Peter is waiting for me in front of a cell where Jerry is angrily pacing back and forth.

"You got no right to hold me, man," Jerry keeps muttering. When Jerry sees me, he rushes to the clear partition. "Cupcake! Tell him I don't belong here."

I raise my eyebrows. "I don't know where you belong, Jerry. I'm not even sure what you are."

He scowls at me and slams his palm against the partition. "I'm a man, Cupcake!"

"Okay," I say, "but are you a man like I'm a woman, or are you just a regular guy? Because I gotta tell you, you don't smell like a regular guy."

He clenches his teeth and steps back from the partition. "This shit again," he mutters.

"What shit is that?" I ask.

"Okay, okay, I was a demon, then I got my soul back. Now I'm a regular guy. Happy? I'm sorry if I still have lingering demon funk. I was one for a long time. Now, let me out of here."

I cock my head and look at him.

He frowns. "Seven thousand souls to my creator. She offered me my soul back, and I accepted."

I raise my eyebrows.

"I know," he says. "It's weird. By that point, most people are more comfortable as demons. They don't know how to go back to being human. I thought I could handle it."

"Are you handling it?" Peter asks.

Jerry glares at him. "Well, I was until someone fucking kidnapped me!"

"So why do you still smell like demon when you get pissed off?" I ask.

He shrugs. "I don't know. I just do."

"So you can't turn back into a demon?"

Jerry levels his gaze at me. "If I could, you'd all be dead."

Big talk from a guy in a box.

Peter frowns. "Let's go," he says to me.

I follow him out as Jerry pounds on the partition behind us. "Come on!" he shouts. "I answered your questions. Let me out of here!"

He continues shouting until we exit the holding area. The thick door closes behind us, and I can't hear Jerry pleading anymore.

"What do you think?" Peter asks.

I sigh. "I'm not sure. What he says is consistent with what I've been told about getting my soul back. I don't think he's lying." I can usually say that with a hundred percent accuracy, but Jerry throws me off a bit. He's hard to read.

Peter blows out a frustrated breath. "I'm going to go back in and talk to him without you. I think as long as you're in there, all he can focus on is trying to get you to talk me into letting him out."

One of the guards walks me back to my room. Wait, scratch that. It isn't my room. It's my cell. It's nicer than it was before, but I'm still being held here. I can't lose sight of that, or I'll end up with Stockholm syndrome. I flop across the bed and stare at the white ceiling tiles. I consider what Peter is looking for. Since I'm fairly certain he autopsied Sugar Pie, I don't understand what he's looking for in trying to MRI or X-ray me. Wouldn't he have learned the answer to what was inside a succubus when he autopsied her?

It turns out I don't have to wait long to ask him. There's a brief knock at my door, and then Peter walks in.

I sit up and lean back against the headboard. "How'd it go with Jerry?"

He frowns and sits on the foot of my bed. "Not that great. He doesn't seem to know any more than you do about the mechanism of being a demon. He never spawned any succubi and dutifully collected souls until he could buy back his own. Although he seems to regret that somewhat."

"Why?"

Peter gave me a sad smile. "He was an incubus for over fifty years. His human friends and family are old or dead now, but he only looks like he's maybe thirty. It's not like he has anything much to put on a resume, so he works as a night clerk in a hotel and helps out demons that need a little human help. He's been saving money for someone to create a false identity for him so he can move on with his life."

I close my eyes and let my head fall back against the wall. "So that's what I have to look forward to when I get my soul back? Just another kind of misery."

"Just because that's been Jerry's experience doesn't mean it has to be yours."

"Really? How's that?"

"Maybe there's a way to exorcise the demon early?"

I roll my eyes. "*The Exorcist* was just a movie. Don't get all weird on me."

"I'm not talking about traditional exorcism. I'm talking about physics."

"Which reminds me, didn't you do an autopsy of Sugar Pie?"

He nods. "Yes."

"So why didn't you get your answers from that? You cut her open. What did you see?"

"She was just a woman. There was nothing strange, no indication she was ever anything but a human female."

"Really?"

I don't understand that. I know Sugar Pie was a succubus. I met her once by accident, and she showed me her true face. I was never early to a meeting with Ian again. As a matter of fact, that was when I started blowing off my meetings with him altogether. Sugar Pie was seriously scary, and she didn't like to share Ian.

"My working theory is that the demon, for lack of a better term, vacates the body when it dies. That was why I was hoping to run tests on a living subject, but I need to come up with better tests, because the ones that work on humans don't work on you."

I shrug. It's not like I'm sad that I can't be his guinea pig.

Sefu walks in. "I've spoken to Jerry."

"Already?" Peter says.

"Yes, given his situation, I thought it prudent to get him out of here as soon as possible."

"What do you mean? You let him go?" Peter seems pretty upset.

All I can muster is curiosity.

"Why?" Peter is on the verge of shouting, but Sefu remains unruffled.

"He's human, Peter. It's hardly ethical to keep him here."

"Right," I say. "It's only ethical to kidnap nonhumans."

Sefu looks at me with those heavy-lidded eyes of his. "You're hardly one to preach ethics."

"Sefu," Peter says.

"It's done," Sefu says. "He's already gone, but we came to a mutually beneficial arrangement before he left."

Of course they did. I can't imagine Sefu does much in the world without getting something in return.

"What arrangement?" Peter asks. He begins pacing in small circles around the room.

Sefu smiles at him. "A good one, Peter. Jerry will be keeping us informed of demon comings and goings."

"And why would he do that?" Peter asks, continuing to pace.

"Because I have agreed to build him a new identity so that he can move beyond his current station in life."

"And how are you going to do that?"

Sefu smiles again, this time with full wattage. "I have my ways. You needn't worry about it, Peter. There is one catch, though."

"What catch?" Peter asks, stopping to look at Sefu.

"He would only consent to talk to Alma. Of course, he calls her Cupcake."

"Me? Why?"

"I think perhaps he doesn't trust us."

"Imagine that," I say.

Sefu smiles again. "It does, however, come with a perk for you."

"What's that?" It bothers me how much I want a perk.

"A phone. Someone will bring it by later."

Chapter 23: Fat TVs and DVDs

Later turns into three hours of me watching old *The X-Files* DVDs. I'd heard of it, but I was never allowed to watch the reruns because Mom felt it was too scary for a little kid. Given my current state, it kind of watches like a situation comedy, and those gigantic brick cell phones are hilarious. I'm totally shipping Mulder and Scully, though.

There's a knock on the door, so I hit Pause, and one of the hazmat suit goons comes in with a phone on a cart. I recognize him by the way he moves, but he's never been on a mission with me, so he's just a goon.

"Phone" is kind of a generous term for it. It's not a cell phone. It's not even cordless. It's a desk model similar to the one my grandmother used to have in her spare room. Where there should be buttons or a dial, though, there's just a solid plate. I guess I'm not allowed to make outgoing calls. The goon plugs it into an old-school phone jack in the wall.

"There you go," he says, all chipper, like I've longed to live like it's 1975.

Although, to be fair, the TV-DVD combo I'm watching is probably more like 1995. Would it kill them to give me access to some decent tech? As soon as the hazmat guy is out the door, I pick up the phone. The handset alone weighs a ton. There's a dial tone but also some suspicious clicking. I'm sure it's bugged. Typical.

Before I can decide whether to return to *The X-Files* or read, another goon comes by to take me to collect another old man's soul. It bothers me that this scenario is starting to feel normal. It's hard not to settle into a rhythm, but I don't want to be too complacent here. It's certainly easier than my previous life as a demon, but what I really want is my previous life as a human. I can't lose sight of that just because things are somewhat better now.

The soul collection goes completely to plan. I arrive at Mr. Chan's room, collect his trash, collect his soul, and roll out with my cart. I don't bother hitting the emergency button, because the machines will alert the nurses' station. I collect the trash from a couple more rooms because there are some other people on the floor. I don't want to draw attention to myself by just booking it to the elevator. I come out of the third room to a clear hallway and return to the elevator. Two goons are waiting for me when I come off the elevator.

"What took so long?"

"I had to clear trash from a couple of extra rooms because there were people in the hall."

"Yeah, all right. Head on back to your room."

The other goon watches me walk down the hall, but he doesn't accompany me. He seems to be the one in charge of the goon squad. Little by little, they trust me more. The problem is, little by little, I trust them more too.

As I open the door to my room, the phone rings. I pick it up.

"Cupcake?"

"Yeah." I'm so used to the nickname now I don't bother to correct him.

"It's Jerry. Can we talk?"

"Sure."

"Not on the phone. In person. I'm sure those bastards are listening in on your phone calls."

"I can ask, man, but it's not like I have a key to the front door."

"I understand. Tell them I want to see you on the National Mall, next to the dinosaur in front of the Natural History Museum."

"Okay. How can I reach you?"

"I'll call you back in an hour."

He hangs up, and I put the receiver back in its cradle.

In a couple of minutes, the phone rings again. It's Sefu. "You can go" is all he says before hanging up, which is how I find myself a few hours later stepping out of the back of a van and walking to the dinosaur in front of the museum. Two of the guys hang back at a discreet distance, their giant guns artfully hidden under trench coats. In the van, they hadn't bothered with full hazmat suits, just gloves and oxygen masks—another sign that they trust me more. Or maybe they knew they were going to follow me in public, and the suits were too much trouble.

Jerry is waiting for me. He looks less ashen than before, and he's wearing jeans and a white T-shirt with a lightweight blue jacket. He slips his arm around my shoulder, and we start walking toward the Washington Monument. My guards trail us but not too closely.

It's a beautiful day on the Mall. The sun is shining. The air is crisp. To anyone walking by, Jerry and I probably look like a nice couple out for a stroll. If only that were the case. Jerry leans in and starts talking quietly in my ear.

"Ian is on a rampage," he says.

"Why?"

"They stole you from him. Plus, they've got those weird guns. Word is he's taking this situation up the chain."

"What chain?" I ask. The demon hierarchy still confuses me. I don't know who Ian is beholden to, if anyone.

"The chain," Jerry says. "Everyone has a boss, Cupcake."

"Okay, so what does that mean?"

"I don't know, but it ain't good. Eventually, you're going to have to choose sides."

I laugh at that. "I have chosen a side. I'm on my side."

"Maybe so, but you'll need to decide which way to go eventually. Aren't you sick of being a caged dog, Cupcake?"

I shake my head. "One master is pretty much like another, Jerry. With Ian, I might have been free to go where I liked, but I had to share my souls with him, and he always left me hungry and hurting. With these people, I don't have freedom, but I don't have to scrounge for souls all the time either. At least I'm well fed."

He shook his head. "Yeah, and have you wondered why they're feeding you so much? What are they fattening you up for?"

I frown at him. "I'm not getting fat."

He rolls his eyes. "Not this you," he says, pinching my arm. "The real you. Aren't you getting bigger?"

Now that he mentions it, I recall thinking my bed seemed smaller the last couple of mornings when I woke up in my true form. I shrug. "Maybe."

"Aren't you wondering why they would want you bigger and stronger? Wouldn't that just make you harder to control should you go rogue on them?"

"I guess."

"Things aren't as they seem, Cupcake."

"Then how are they?" I ask, irritated by his cryptic tone.

"That guy, Peter, you know he's not on your team."

I laugh. Like I care that Peter's gay. "I know."

He looks at me incredulously. "That doesn't bother you?"

"No."

He stops and steps away and stares at me. "You're a demon, Cupcake."

"Yeah." I really have no idea what he's talking about. Are demons supposed to have something against gay people?

We're down by the National Museum of American History now. I wonder how long it's been since I've been in there. Probably a school trip. Eighth grade, maybe.

"But I don't want to be one. I'm sick of other people making decisions for me."

"That's just it, though. Decisions are being made."

I frown at him. I'm sick of his cryptic crap. "If you're trying to make a point, I'm missing it. Say what you dragged me out here to say."

He sighs and shakes his head. "There's no point. You're a baby, and you're making decisions with your stomach instead of your head."

"I might be a baby demon, but I'm a grown woman, and I know a manipulative guy when I see one. Right now, I'm surrounded by them, so if you don't have any useful information, you're wasting my time."

"I'm just saying you can't trust those guys. Look at them back there. What do you think they would do to you if you just took off?"

I roll my eyes. "They'd track me down, exactly like Ian is trying to do. So yeah, I can't trust them. I also can't trust Ian, or you, for that matter."

"I'm trying to help you."

"Yeah? How? By talking in riddles and doing fuck all for me. That's not very helpful."

"Ian's trying to figure a way to break you out."

"Tell him not to bother. He doesn't want to mess with these guys. Or he'll end up like Sugar Pie."

"I have told him that. He's not listening."

"Then I guess we'll see how it goes." I don't feel as confident as I sound. This entire encounter has me more confused than I was before.

Jerry shakes his head and walks away.

The goons move in closer. I ignore them and walk to the van. For a fleeting second, I consider trying to escape, but the odds are against my surviving that plan, so I get in the back of the van.

I don't speak to anyone on the ride back to the facility. My mind is racing, and I feel as trapped as I did when I was first captured.

Chapter 24: Assassination

When we arrive back at the facility, I'm taken to Sefu's office instead of my room. Sefu sits behind his big mahogany desk. He gestures for me to sit in one of the chairs in front of him. He smiles at me.

"So, what did Jerry have to say?"

"Apparently, Ian is very pissed and has decided to take his case up the chain."

Sefu arches an eyebrow at me. "What does that mean?"

"I have no idea."

"You don't know anything about the demon hierarchy?"

"Nope. I only know Ian."

He frowns.

I'm careful to keep my expression neutral. I'm not sure what's going on or what I want to do, so while I'm trying to figure that out, I don't want to push anything.

"What about Jerry? Does he know?"

I sigh and look at the soapstone hippopotamus that sits on the edge of Sefu's desk. "Probably, but he wasn't interested in explaining it to me. My experience with demons is that they don't say much directly. Everything is half statements and riddles."

"That's unfortunate," Sefu says. He follows my gaze. "Did you know that the hippo is the most dangerous animal in all of Africa? More human deaths are attributed to it than any other animal."

I look up at him. "Even man?"

He smiles again. "Except man. Which reminds me. I have a special job for you."

All the alarm bells go off in my head.

"What job?"

"There is a man coming to this hospital for an operation on his heart. It's important that he not leave here alive."

I shift in my chair. "Sounds personal."

"It is."

"Sure. Just tell me when and who I'm supposed to look like."

"It will be tonight. His security will be very tight, so you'll need to impersonate his wife. We will keep his actual wife discreetly detained for a few minutes. He also travels with a man who will recognize you for what you are. We will arrange for him to be out of the building."

"Sounds complicated."

Sefu nods. "But not for you. You may go. Someone will be by to collect you later."

I stand to go but then consider what I got the last time I did one of his special assignments and turn around. "I want to see my mom again."

"Kill this man, and I'll see to it."

There are guards in the hallways, but I'm allowed to walk unaccompanied back to my room. So I'm an assassin now. "Succubus assassin" sounds absurd, but I guess that's as good a description as any.

Peter is waiting for me when I get back to my room. He's sitting on my bed with a stack of paperbacks and a handful of DVDs beside him.

"Hi." I consider what Jerry said about Peter not being on my team and reconsider. Maybe Jerry was referring to Peter being a priest. I suppose priests are the natural enemies of demons.

"I brought you some things to read and to watch. Sefu said you were running low."

I pick up the DVDs and look through them. *The Blue Planet*, *Rumpole of the Bailey*, *The Ascent of Man*. "Are these yours?"

He shakes his head. "Not your taste?"

I shrug. "In here, everything is my taste." I look at the books. They're all old science fiction titles: *The Space Merchants*, *The October Country*, *Solaris*, *Foundation*, *Imperial Earth*. "Thanks for these." I wonder where this stuff comes from. I get why the DVDs are old, but would it kill them to get me a couple of novels written in this century? "It was nice of you to bring them."

"You're welcome," he says, standing.

I decide to throw a little caution to the wind. "Hey, can I ask you a weird question?"

"Sure."

"Do you hate me?"

Peter's eyebrows shoot up in surprise. "No. Why would I?"

"You're a priest. I'm a demon. I feed on the souls of men."

He lets out a soft snort. "You house a demon that feeds on the souls of men, but I don't believe that's who you are. And I'm certain you didn't choose the situation you're in, so I don't hate you. I want to help you."

"How?"

"By figuring out how this was done to you and reversing it."

In spite of myself, I feel a certain thrill of possibility. "You can do that?"

"Not yet, but if my theories are correct, it should be possible."

"And if your theories aren't correct?"

"Then I'll need new theories." He smiles that annoying little smile of his. "Good night, Alma."

When the door closes behind him, I flop onto my bed and stare at the ceiling, trying to remember what little I know about religion. Sunday school was a long time ago. I only went for a few years when I was little, when my father was still in the army and my mother and I lived with my grandparents. I can remember coloring pictures of Jesus and his disciples and of angels talking to shepherds, but they certainly never talked about demons. I'm desperate for internet access. I want to look up priests and demons and quantum physics and try to connect what all that means, but I don't have the internet. All I have is a fat TV and some old DVDs. Frustrated, I pop in *The Blue Planet*, hoping that watching the ocean will be soothing. Unfortunately, the picture quality is crap. It's not so obtrusive on the old TV shows, but I've seen *Blue Planet II*, so I know how beautiful it would be on a nice big flat-screen.

Two hours later, I've had all the nature I can stand and click off the TV when someone knocks on the door. A new goon hands me the nicest clothes I've ever seen in real life. He also hands me several pictures of who I'm supposed to be. Her height, weight, and measurements are included on the back of the photo. It only takes me a minute to transform into her, but I stop and take a moment to appreciate the Chanel suit of ivory silk jacquard that they've brought me. It probably costs roughly what my mother makes in a month. It's super nice and surprisingly comfortable. The ivory looks fantastic against the deep-ebony skin of the woman I've turned into. I stand looking at the full-length mirror for so long that one of the goons knocks on the door and tells me to hurry up. I slip on a pair of silk Prada pumps that match the dress perfectly and step out of my room. One of the regular goons is waiting with the new goon.

"Let's go," the new goon barks, and we head for the elevator.

I'm surprised to find two additional goons in the elevator. They're familiar, although I've never seen them in gray jumpsuits without respirators before. I take a deep breath, drawing in their scents so I will know them in the future.

"Here's what's going to happen," one of them says as the elevator door closes. "We're going to take you up to the fifth floor. When I get the signal, you're going to go to room 514 and do your thing. When you're done, you come right back to me. Understood?"

"Sure," I say.

"There's going to be a guard at the door, but he should let you right through because he's going to think you're the guy's wife. If he should say something, like good evening or whatnot, keep your response minimal. Got that?"

"Minimal. Got it," I say. This guy must think I'm an idiot.

"This is a quick in and out. Don't linger."

I glare at him. "I never linger."

"Right."

They both seem nervous. The new goon actually has beads of sweat on his forehead, and he keeps wiping his brow with a handkerchief. The others just seem antsy. I can't decide whether they're nervous about the op or about being in an elevator with me. It's probably a toss-up.

When we arrive on the fifth floor, the guards usher me around a corner. About a minute later, a small group wearing traditional African garb walks by and gets on the elevator.

"Do your thing," the goon in charge tells me.

I roll my eyes at him and walk down the hall toward room 514. It's easy to find, since it's the only room with a guard standing in front of it. The guy is at least six foot one, with broad shoulders and a menacing scar down the side of his face. He's wearing black tactical clothing, and although I don't see a gun on him, I feel sure there is one.

He holds his palm up as I approach the room. "What are you doing here?" he asks quietly.

His accent is melodious like Sefu's, which seems incongruous coming from such a tough-looking guy. I don't know enough about African countries to place the accent, but I wish I knew where he was from so I would know a little more about Sefu.

"I'm here to say good night to my husband," I reply, mimicking his accent.

He snorts. "Right," he says with a smile.

Uh-oh. I'm thinking maybe this situation isn't what I was led to believe, but the guard seems nice. I can smell his attraction to the woman I'm imitating. I give him a sexy smile.

He smiles back. "You know I can't let you in there," he says in a deep, velvety voice.

I look up at him coyly. "Maybe I'm just here to see you. I saw the others leaving."

He grins slyly. "I can't leave my post."

I slide up to him, pressing my body against his. "So a little something to hold me over," I whisper.

He glances to the left and right, making sure the hall is empty before tilting his head down. I slide my hands up and pull his face down to me for a kiss.

He relaxes into it and opens his mouth. I suck out his soul with little effort. He struggles for just a second, but I'm stronger than he is, which is a good thing, because he's suddenly dead weight, literally. I hold him with one arm, open the door with my other hand, and press us both into the room as quickly as I can. There is a bathroom just inside the room, so holding him up with one arm, I unbuckle his belt and drop his pants with the other. I stuff him into the bathroom and set him on the toilet before closing the door.

The guy in the bed was dozing when I came in, but now he's wide awake and sitting up. He says something to me in French, but I don't speak French. He sounds alarmed.

I shrug.

His eyes widen. He shouts something at me and reaches for the call button to bring a nurse.

I grab his hand. "I don't think so." I advance on him and grab his face. He struggles, but he's weak from whatever his condition is. I take his soul and am startled by the difference between his and the guard's. This guy's soul is weak and atrophied. The guard's is big and fills my belly.

Alarm bells start to go off on all the monitors when the guy dies. Shit. I can hear the code team hurrying down the hall with the crash cart. I run out into the hall and shout, "It's my husband. Help him, help him!"

The team tears past me while I slip down the hall toward the guards, who hurry me onto the elevator.

Sefu is waiting for us when the elevator opens. "What have you done? You weren't supposed to kill the guard!"

"I didn't have a choice. He wouldn't let me in. I guess your pal and his wife aren't exactly on friendly terms."

Sefu shook his head. "But why did you have to kill him?"

"What did you want me to do? I'm a succubus, not a ninja. I have two options. Kill or ignore."

He runs a frustrated hand down his forehead. "Never mind. We have to get you out of here."

"Why?"

He ignores me and turns to the goons. "Get the away team geared up. Both vans, both guns. And you," he says to the new goon, "get her a change of clothes quickly and get to the van."

"What's going on?"

"We have to get you out of here."

"Why?"

"I told you. He travels with a dangerous man. He's off grounds right now, but he'll be informed of the death and come back. He'll sense you're here, so you can't be here."

Peter walks up. "What's happened?"

"I need you to cover for Alma's exit."

"Right." Peter nods and walks off.

"How is he going to cover my exit?"

"I don't have time to explain that now."

The two familiar elevator guards hurry me down the hall toward the garage. "Take her to her mother's house," Sefu shouts after us. "I'll contact you when you can bring her back."

I climb into the van, and the goons follow. I'm elated at the idea of being able to see my mother again but also irritated at being pushed out the door without an explanation. The goon who was tasked to bring me a change of clothes runs up, throws in a gym bag, and climbs in, pulling the doors shut behind him. The van takes off.

"Get changed," says the guy in charge, who I've started to think of as Bay Rum because of his cologne. I've given all the goons names based on their scents. The guard who got my clothes is Axe, and the other guard is Ocean because his aftershave smells salty. I call the driver Goldy because he uses Gold Bond powder. Goldy and Bay Rum are the guards who sometimes play cards with me. They're my favorites.

"Get changed," Axe says gruffly.

I grab the bag of clothes. Bay Rum and Ocean avert their eyes. Axe continues staring.

"You mind?" I say pointedly.

"Rules are we don't take our eyes off you."

I glare at him. "Fine."

When I was in college, I took a twentieth-century history class and wrote a paper on leper colonies. During my research, I came across a photo of an old woman with advanced leprosy. I take my shirt off and turn into her. Axe scrambles backward across the van. He looks like he might vomit. Bay Rum and Ocean laugh at him. I finish changing and turn back into my original appearance.

"Girl, that was rough," Ocean says, grinning.

I laugh.

Chapter 25: Reed

Two hours later, the van pulls up just down the street from my mother's place. The other van circles around to the street behind the house.

"You know the drill," Bay Rum says.

"Yes. I'll behave. How long do I have?"

"No idea, I'll come get you when it's time."

"That's going to be hard to explain to my mother."

He shrugs. "I'd tell you more if I knew more."

"Great."

He pushes open the door for me, and I step into the sunshine. A gentle breeze is blowing, and I take a moment just to soak it up before walking to my mother's house. There's a strange car in her driveway. As I approach, I see it has California plates. That's weird. I don't recall my mother ever having friends over. I know she likes some of the people she works with and occasionally goes for a drink with them on Friday evenings. Maybe now that I'm not home, she's having people over.

I try the doorknob, and it's unlocked. I open the door and stick my head in. Someone is laughing in the kitchen. I can smell chocolate chip cookies fresh from the oven.

"Hey, Mom, are you here?"

"Alma!" my mother cries out. She actually runs to the door.

I step all the way inside, and she hugs me.

"Oh, Alma! It's so good to see you." She holds me tight for a moment and then steps back. "You'll never guess who's here."

"Hey, Alma," a familiar voice says, and Reed Johnson steps into the hallway.

I open my mouth to say something, but all the words seem to have fallen out of my head. I can't believe he's here. Reed is the first man I ever loved. Although, to be fair, he was really more of a boy when I loved him, though he certainly seems to be all man now. We broke up when we were seventeen, halfway through our senior year of high school, when his mother got transferred to Nevada for her job. Until I met Ian, Reed had been the only guy I'd ever slept with. The only guy I'd ever even kissed.

Reed Johnson is standing in my living room, and I still haven't said anything. I manage to squeak out, "Reed."

He hugs me, and it feels so good. And then I remember I'm a succubus just as his cheek grazes mine. Oh shit! I step away from him, but I know it's already too late. I just tagged him with tracking pheromones. Now wherever Reed goes, I'll know where he is. What am I going to do? How does that work if I'm not hunting someone? Does it wear off eventually? I've never tested to see how long it lasts.

"Come in the kitchen," my mother says. "I just made chocolate chip cookies."

"Yum," I say, smiling. But inside, I'm panicking big-time. I've never tagged a man and then not eaten his soul. When I've done it before, I was obsessed with the guy until I finished him off. It's kind of like the worst craving in the world. This is not good.

We sit down at the kitchen table, and my mom gets us all glasses of milk before setting a plate of cookies in the middle of the table. It's like we're twelve again and Reed has come over after school to work on a class project. He smells so good. I close my eyes for a second and try not to think of his smell as delicious.

"Reed arrived just before you did," my mother says, obviously delighted. "He had just started telling me what brought him back to the East Coast."

I smile at him.

"I'm starting at George Mason in a couple of weeks."

The math on that doesn't make sense to me, and it must show on my face.

"I took a couple of years to work odd jobs and get my associate's degree, but now I'm ready to finish up my bachelor's. Mason has a really good public policy program."

I nod and smile, but all I can think about is his thick dark hair and his olive skin. His shirt is doing justice to his biceps as he leans over the table to get another cookie. The Johnsons adopted Reed from Korea when he was a baby, so despite his WASP name, he's all Korean and a big guy to boot. He was the only Korean guy on our football team in high school. I could just eat him up. Quite literally.

"Alma was at GMU," my mother says and then instantly covers her mouth with her hand.

"Was?" Reed asks.

"I'm taking a break," I say smoothly.

Reed tilts his head at me and smiles. "A break? That doesn't sound like you."

My mother makes a little strangled noise in the back of her throat.

I pat her hand. "It's okay, Mom."

She grimaces, and a tear slips from her right eye. "I'll let you two catch up," she chokes out and hurries from the room.

"What was that about?" Reed asks, concern etched across his face.

"I had a little trouble with drugs. There was this guy. It's a long, ugly story. Suffice it to say I'm better now. I'm in a program. It's working. I'm not my father, but that's what she's afraid of."

"Wow, Alma."

I shrug and smile. "It's my own fault, but I'm better. I'll go back to school when I'm done with the program."

"When will that be?"

"Oh, you know, I'm taking it one day at a time."

He nods. "Oh, sure, sure."

I'm glad he bought that. I don't know that many clichés about recovery. My dad never bothered with it. He just drank and drugged himself to death, and that was that.

"Well, you look great," he adds.

I smile at him. "You too," I say without thinking, and then I kick myself. No matter how much I would like to, this thing with Reed must not be rekindled. I'm incredibly eager to leave even though I just got here.

Reed takes another cookie and leans back in his chair like he's settling in for a long talk. The urge to kiss him and take his soul is nearly overwhelming. I've never been in a situation like this, and I don't know what to do.

My mother comes back into the room. "Reed, can you stay for lunch?"

He smiles. "Sure. I'd love that."

I smile, too, but it's not great. It's terrible.

There's a knock on the front door.

My mother answers it, and I can hear one of the goons say it's time to go. He follows my mother into the kitchen like a looming shadow. It's Bay Rum, in regular street clothes. I've never seen him like that. In some ways, it's scarier than the hazmat suit.

"Hey, Alma, we need to get back." He eyes Reed and looks at me with a scowl on his face.

"So soon?" my mother says to me. "You just got here."

I smile at her. "I'm sorry, Mom. This wasn't really a scheduled visit. We were on an outing nearby, and I asked if I could pop in and see you. I'm doing well, so they said yes."

Bay Rum nods. "We're very pleased with Alma's progress." He says it smoothly, going along with the lie, but his voice is so deep and he's such a big guy that he's not exactly selling it.

I kiss my mother's cheek. "I've got to go. I love you."

She hugs me. "I love you too."

Reed follows Bay Rum and me to the door. "I guess I'll see you around."

I smile at him. "I hope so." But I hope not. I've got to stay far, far away from him until these pheromones wear off. If they wear off.

I leave him and my mother standing on the stoop of her little brick house. They both look sad and confused as I get into the van. I've never been so happy to drive to Baltimore in my life.

Bay Rum is getting back into his hazmat suit. I look at him and frown. "I'm not going to hurt you."

He nods and pulls the hood up. "I know, but what if we have an accident? I don't want to accidentally touch you. You're passively dangerous as well as actively dangerous. I can't forget that just because I'm used to you."

I nod. "Right." No kidding.

I hope Sefu has a solution to my Reed problem, because I'm already aching for him. The desire to break through the back of the van and go hunting is very strong. I take deep breaths and lean back in my seat. I never thought I would ever be happy to be locked inside the facility, but I want that more than anything right now.

"Who was that guy?" Bay Rum asks me.

"Just someone that I used to know."

He frowns at me. "You're not supposed to have unauthorized contact with men."

"He was there when I got there. I couldn't exactly ask him to leave."

"I'll have to report it to Sefu."

I shrug. "Fine. I was going to tell him myself." My skin feels like it's on fire.

Sefu is waiting for us when we arrive.

"We've got a problem," I say as I get out of the van. I'm having trouble standing still. I don't know what to do with my hands.

Bay Rum follows me and stands next to me as the others put their gear away.

"What now?" Sefu says, clearly exasperated.

"I had unintentional contact with a man."

Sefu glares at Bay Rum. "How did that happen?"

"It's no one's fault," I say. "He was visiting my mother when I arrived."

Sefu's lips tighten as he looks at Bay Rum and then back to me. "In my office."

Bay Rum starts to follow, but Sefu holds up a palm to him. "Not you. I'll deal with you later."

Sefu closes the door behind us and points at one of the chairs in front of his desk, but I don't sit down. I can't sit down.

"What's wrong with you?" Sefu asks, frowning at me.

"Didn't you hear me? I touched a man."

"And?" Sefu says.

"And? And I'm linked to him now!" I can't help shouting.

"Linked? Why did you use pheromones on him?"

"I didn't use them. It just happens."

"You don't have control over who you tag?"

"No."

Sefu arches an eyebrow at me. "Really? That's not my understanding of how it works."

"Well, I can't help your understanding. It's what happened. What are we going to do?" I'm pacing the room, trying not to panic.

"Calm down, Alma. I'm sure Peter will have some ideas."

"Will he?" I ask. "Because this is a nightmare."

Sefu opens the door and gestures toward Ocean. "Escort her down to the lab."

Peter is sitting at his desk, staring at a computer screen when we arrive. Ocean leaves without a word, and once again, I'm struck that no one minds leaving me with Peter unattended. It's probably just the pheromones talking, but I have a desperate urge to put my hands on Peter just to see what would happen.

He stands, clearing his throat as he does, and I manage to control myself.

"I understand you've had quite the day."

"Yeah, you could say that."

Peter smiles sympathetically. "So you've tagged a man with pheromones without meaning to?"

"Yes, they took me to my mother's house, and an old boyfriend of mine was there visiting her. He's just moved back to the area. He hugged me."

Peter scratches at his late-day stubble and seems to be thinking. "Have you ever tagged someone and then not gone after them?"

"No."

"Any idea how long the pheromones last?"

"No. I haven't tagged that many guys, and I always caught up to the ones I did within a few hours."

"And how are you feeling now?"

I'm not as itchy as I had been in the van. "Actually, I feel a bit better. It was awful in the van, though."

"The van doesn't have massive air filters scrubbing the air. You shouldn't be able to smell your prey in here, and in a couple of days the pheromone should wear off—assuming he showers daily."

I drop down into one of the lab chairs and blow out a sigh of relief. "Fantastic. That's great news." My mind is racing. This also explains why it's so difficult to identify the guards by smell in the facility but so easy when we're outside.

Peter sits back down in his own chair and rolls toward me. "Tell me, what did you do to rate a trip home today?"

I'm thrown off guard. I assumed he knew since he'd been called in to cover my exit. "Um."

He smiles at me again. "I'm not trying to put you in an awkward position, but Sefu asked me to do something quite dangerous today. Since I know he would never ask such a thing lightly, there must've been something very serious going on, but for some reason, I've been kept in the dark."

"You should probably ask Sefu," I say. My mind is racing with what this might mean.

"I'm asking you, Alma."

I'm really torn. On the one hand, I like Peter, but I'm scared of crossing Sefu. "I don't want to make waves. My predecessor wound up dead. I don't want to make the same mistake."

"Her death was an unfortunate accident. It wasn't done to her out of some sort of retaliation."

I shake my head. "Maybe that's true, and maybe it's not, but if Sefu didn't tell you what I did today, I think that probably means I shouldn't either."

He frowns at me. Then his face relaxes. "I'm sorry. I shouldn't put you in the middle of this. Don't worry about it. You can go back to your room now."

As I open the door to leave, Peter says, "And, Alma..."

I turn to look at him.

"Have a good night."

He walks away from me and enters one of the side rooms in the lab. Something about the way he wishes me good night feels like a threat, but I'm not sure why. I'm starting to think maybe Sefu isn't the only one I shouldn't cross around here. Jerry clearly thinks Peter is a problem, maybe even a bigger problem than Sefu, and I have zero desire to be in the middle of whatever those two are arguing about.

When I get back to my room, I let my human form drop and stand looking at myself in the full-length mirror that was installed on the bathroom door when I started regularly turning into hospital staff to take souls. I'm definitely taller and not the same pastel-pink color that

I used to be. I'm a darker rose color now, and the little buds that were my horns are now a little longer. I certainly look like a demon, but I still feel like Alma. Seeing Reed today really reinforced both of those things.

In an attempt to shift my focus from the desire to hunt Reed, I go over the day's events that led to seeing Reed in the first place. Clearly, the guy I killed this morning was a big deal, and Sefu obviously has some kind of connection to him. I wonder if the death will make the paper, but if it does, I'm guessing I won't get that paper. It's not like they bring me a newspaper every day. Maybe I shouldn't have made that crack about the *Sun* vs. the *Post*. To be honest, aside from my mother, what I miss most is my phone. I never realized just how much I used it for everything. My current inability to look up any piece of information whenever I want to makes me a little crazy.

I want to know who the guy I killed last night was, which is kind of weird because generally, I absolutely don't want to know who my victims are. It makes me feel less like a monster if I can keep them at arm's length so they feel like food instead of people, kind of like people who have pet chickens but still eat chicken. It's complicated, but it works for me. Sort of. Anyway, I want to know who that guy was and where he was from and how he connects to Sefu—all of which might be available with a simple internet search.

Then there's Peter. What did Peter do that covered my exit, and why was it dangerous? Sefu said the man I killed traveled with a dangerous man. Dangerous to whom? Me? Sefu? Both? What had Ian said about demon hunters? Priests, witch doctors, and physicists. I wonder which the dangerous guy is. Unfortunately, I've got absolutely no way of figuring any of this out without resources. The itch to hunt goes crawling up my spine again.

The night is long, and sleep is elusive. I keep remembering moments in my relationship with Reed: playing flag football with friends, riding around in his dad's old pickup truck, laughing while we played

Mario Kart, camping, our first kiss, the first time he said he loved me. I've missed him, but I'm going to have to avoid him like the plague. Only, I don't need to avoid the actual plague. If some guy showed up at the hospital with bubonic plague, I'd probably end up eating his soul.

I hate my life.

Chapter 26: Pheromones

At six o'clock in the morning, Sefu walks in without knocking just like he always does. This morning, I find that exceptionally irritating, especially since he doesn't have a newspaper with him.

He raises his eyebrows. "Not feeling very human this morning, Alma?"

I'm still in demon form as I get out of bed. "Not particularly." I decide not to switch my form just to annoy him. I like that he has to look up to me when I'm this shape.

"That's fine for now, but I expect you to look human later when the trainer arrives."

"What trainer?" I'm curious despite my irritation.

"We can't have any more incidents like the one that happened yesterday."

"I told you I didn't touch him. He touched me."

Sefu shook his head. "Not that. That's an easy fix. I'm talking about you killing the security guard."

I open my mouth to protest, but he raises a hand to stop me.

"I know. You only have two options right now, but that will change. The trainer will make sure you can incapacitate someone without killing them. She will teach you to use your strength more effectively. Also, along those same lines, Peter has some tests he'd like to run this morning before the trainer arrives. Do me a favor—make like a human before you walk down to the lab. He's ready when you are." With that, he turns and walks out.

He's getting pretty comfortable letting me walk around the facility by myself, which works in my favor, but to what end? Without a steady diet of dying men, I'll be right back where I was before. What I need is a solution that sets me free, not one that just trades Ian for Sefu. I let that concept swim around in my mind while I resume my human form and get dressed. For a moment, I amuse myself by thinking about what would happen if I strolled down to Peter's office in full succubus mode. It's fun to consider, but I'm not willing to press my luck around here. This cage might be increasingly gilded, but it's still a cage.

As I walk down the hall to Peter's lab, I can't see a way out that doesn't land me back with Ian. If my choice is to not share souls and get stronger or share souls and stay weak, I know which one is my preference.

When I walk into the lab, it looks different. Equipment I've never seen before is set up around the room.

"New toys?" I ask Peter.

He smiles. "Yes. Today, I'd like to test your strength and reflexes."

"Fine."

He gestures toward one of the new pieces of equipment while he types something on one of the lab computers. "Can you punch that pad as hard as you can?"

I punch the pad without giving it much thought, and the computer chimes.

"Wow," Peter says.

"How'd I do?"

"Eighteen hundred pounds per square inch."

"Is that a lot?"

"For the average human, yes. For a heavyweight boxer, also yes."

The rest of the morning is spent testing me. I feel like I'm trying to pass a souped-up version of the Presidential Fitness Test from elementary school. It turns out I can run thirty-five miles an hour but only for a few minutes. I can deadlift 1,600 pounds without straining. My vertical leap is seven feet. I wonder if all this information is for the trainer. I've never really tested my abilities. I did throw that motorcycle at Ian, but I'm not sure how much a Harley weighs. It wasn't difficult to throw, though.

Peter looks at his watch. "That's enough for today, Alma. Very impressive."

One of the hazmat goons opens the lab door and sticks his helmeted head in. "Sefu wants you in the training room. Come on," he says to me.

I glance at Peter before following. Peter's expression is difficult to read, but it seems disapproving to me.

I follow the hazmat guy down the hall in the opposite direction from my room. Since I can't see his face, I play a little guessing game as to who I'm dealing with. I can't smell him, and his voice is filtered, so he sounds tinny. I watch the way he moves. He's quiet, too, which is also a clue. I think it's Ocean.

When we reach the end of the hall, Sefu is waiting for me. He stares at me for a moment. "You should look more muscular, leaner."

I adjust my physique. "Why?"

He gestures for me to open one of a set of double doors that lead into a large open room that's been kitted out like a gym. The floor is mostly covered in thick blue vinyl mats like the kind they had in gym class at school. A tall woman with short dark curly hair is standing in the middle of the room. She's wearing a black tank top, camouflage cargo pants, and black combat boots. Her arms and shoulders are muscular, and she looks like she might be able to take Sefu in a fight.

"Alma," Sefu says. "This is Maddy Hoffman. She's going to train you in Krav Maga self-defense tactics."

I look at Sefu and then at Maddy and then back at Sefu. Surely, he's joking. "Can I speak to you a moment?"

"Of course." He turns to Maddy. "Excuse us."

"Sure," she says.

I follow Sefu back out into the hallway. He closes the door behind us. "What's the problem?"

I glare at him. "Uh, I don't know. This is stupid."

"You told me you killed the guard because you only had one tool at your disposal. This will give you alternatives."

"You want that tiny woman to train a demon how to use Krav Maga, seriously?"

"She doesn't know you're a demon."

"What does she think I am?"

"A test subject."

"For what kind of test?"

"Medical fitness, effectiveness of various workouts over time, et cetera," Sefu says, waving his hand dismissively.

I raise my eyebrows in disbelief. "And she bought that?"

Sefu sighs. "We pay well."

I frown. "You must. Too bad I'm not seeing any of that compensation."

"Yes, well, at least you're not dead." He says it casually, but I hear the threat loud and clear.

"Right. Have you gotten the results of Peter's tests yet? Apparently, I pack a pretty mean punch."

He cocks his head, and I realize what I said also sounded threatening.

"I'm just saying she'll probably notice I'm freakishly strong."

"Yes. You'll have to hold back."

I roll my eyes. "Don't squish her. I get it."

Sefu frowns but opens the door for me to return to the trainer while he stands in the corner of the room, watching.

I approach Maddy and stick out my hand. "Sorry about that. I'm Alma."

She shakes my hand and smiles. "No worries. Are you ready for this?"

I smile back. "I guess."

Holding back proves to be harder than I anticipated. It's very complicated to hold my human shape and modulate my speed and strength at the same time. Maddy takes me through a series of holds and throws. When it's my turn to demonstrate what she shows me, it's hard not to throw her across the room. A couple of times, I slip and am too rough, but she bounces back to her feet and smiles every time. "Very good," she says. "You've had martial arts training before."

"I took tae kwon do as a kid. Jhoon Rhee was big where I grew up."

She chuckles. "You must've had a very good instructor."

I shrug. "I liked him."

Actually, that part is sort of true. I took tae kwon do at Jhoon Rhee studio in Fairfax for a few months when I was ten years old. They were running a special on classes, and I talked my parents into letting me go. I really did like the instructor. He was nice, and I remember thinking he was cute. He was just a kid himself, probably no more than twenty. Increasingly, memories like that feel like they belong to someone else, like I knew that little girl but she wasn't really me. I can't help wondering if that sensation is my humanity slipping away. The thought leaves me with a knot in my stomach.

"I think that's enough for today. We don't want to overdo it. I'll see you tomorrow," Maddy says.

"Oh, okay." I'm not even remotely tired, but I guess I would be if I were human. "We're doing this every day, then?"

"Yep, for the next two weeks. Didn't they tell you?"

"Oh, right, yeah, of course. They did say something about that when I signed up for this." I know that was a pretty weak response, but I couldn't think of anything else to say.

Maddy smiles. "Okay. Tomorrow, then."

"Yep."

Sefu is no longer watching as I walk back to the gym door. I don't know when he left. A guard is waiting to escort me back to my room.

There wasn't a clock in the gym, so I'm surprised when I get back to my room to find we'd been at it for three hours. I'm not even sore. One of the perks of being a monster, I suppose.

Chapter 27: A Phone Call

I'm watching *Rumpole of the Bailey* and lamenting the poor production values when the phone rings. I turn off the TV and pick up the handset. "Hello?"

"Alma?" my mother says.

"Hi, Mama." I sit up. "Is everything okay?"

"I was calling to ask you that."

"I'm fine."

"I was worried that seeing Reed might've upset you."

She has no idea how true that is. "I'm okay. I wish the circumstances had been different, but it is what it is." Vague is my best position in any conversation with my mother.

"I want you to know I didn't invite him over. He just stopped by." I can hear the anxiety in her voice.

"It's okay. Of course he stopped by. Why wouldn't he?"

"I just don't want this to set you back. I know how upset you were when he left."

"Yeah, but that was a while ago. A lot has happened since then. I'm not going to fall apart just because Reed is back in Northern Virginia. It's not like we've kept in touch."

"All right. I just wanted to check in. I'm not trying to upset you."

"You're not. I like that you checked in. You don't have to worry about me. I'm doing really well here."

"I just want you to succeed."

"I know."

"That man that came to the house was kind of scary."

"He's really a sweetheart, a gentle giant." He's not, but she doesn't need to know that.

"Good, because—"

"I know, he's huge. Listen, they're telling me I need to go. We've got a group meeting."

"Okay. I won't keep you. I love you."

"Love you too." I set the handset back in its cradle and stare at the old phone. I hated to cut the conversation short, but I don't want to talk about fake rehab or Reed. Truth be told, if I wasn't a succubus trapped in a hospital basement prison, if I was still in college, I would be thrilled that Reed was back. Even more so that he was going to George Mason. Reed is one of the best people I've ever known, and if he wanted to rekindle things with me, I'd be all for giving us another try. Unfortunately, there can't be an us, because I'm not really me anymore, and I don't know how to fix that. I lean forward, resting my head in my hands. A tear rolls down my cheek and hits the floor with a sizzle, illustrating perfectly the futility of my situation.

Sighing, I fall back against the bed and turn the TV back on. Clearly, the BBC didn't spend any money on these old shows. The audio is completely uneven, and everything on set, including the actors, is a variation of beige. The stories are good, though. I'd prefer something considerably more current, but it beats nothing.

The phone rings again, awaking me from a nap. I nap a lot these days. I reach for the handset and hold it to my ear without saying anything. I'm expecting it to be Sefu telling me I have an assignment.

"Alma?"

"Reed?"

"Hey, I hope it's okay that I called. Your mom gave me the number."

"Oh, yeah, sure." My mind is racing. I know they listen in on my phone calls. Why would they even have put Reed through? What are they expecting to learn?

"I just wanted you to know that it was really great seeing you. I'm sorry about your situation, but I'm really impressed that you're getting help. Not everyone does."

"I know. Dad didn't, and I don't want to end up like him."

"You won't." Reed says it so earnestly that I feel myself tear up.

"Thanks," I choke out.

"I really would like to catch up sometime."

"That would be great," I say in spite of myself. I know it won't happen.

He gives me the number to his cell phone. I scratch it into the top of the dresser with one of my claws even though I know I'll never call. Not that I could if I wanted to. My phone doesn't have a keypad.

When I hang up the phone, I feel worse than before. I lie back down, not bothering to hold my human shape. What's the point? I'm a monster.

I must've dozed off again, because a sharp rap on my door wakes me. One of the goons comes in—I'm not sure which one, because he's in full hazmat gear, and I don't feel like guessing.

"They need you upstairs." He hands me a new badge with the photo of a Hispanic woman who works in food services. That's new. I usually pretend to work in waste disposal.

He closes the door behind him, and I transform into the woman and get dressed.

I walk down to the elevator unaccompanied. Instead of a cleaning cart, one of those big rolling carts that holds multiple trays of food is waiting for me. It's empty. Bay Rum is in the elevator. He's not wearing protective gear. I push the cart into the elevator, and he presses the button for the lobby.

"Room 612 is your target. You can leave the cart on the sixth floor."

"Okay."

I do the elevator change by myself, realizing as I do so that it's morning. I lose all track of time downstairs. I wonder if anyone notices that the food cart isn't coming from the kitchen, but no one gives me a second glance as I cross the lobby to the other bank of elevators. Sighing, I push the button for the sixth floor. I start down the hall for room 612. A wall of windows on one side of the hall catches my attention, and I stop to take in the view. It's just the parking deck, but it's outside and open, so it looks inviting. I'm hungry, but I don't want to kill anyone today. Not that I ever really want to, but today, I'm especially sick of my situation.

A helicopter comes in for a landing on top of the parking deck, but it isn't marked like a rescue helicopter or a police helicopter. It's plain black. No ER team rushes to meet it. Curious, I stay and watch. Two grim-faced men in business suits exit the copter and start toward the rooftop entrance. One man is tall and dark-skinned. His short haircut, high cheekbones, and closely trimmed goatee remind me of Sefu. The other man is shorter, dark haired, and olive skinned. Something about him makes me think he's Eastern European. Regardless of where the two are from, an icy chill runs down my spine, and I know I have to get out of here. I forget about my mission and run back to the elevator. When the doors don't immediately open, I run for the stairs. I'm not sure why I feel so panicked, but I've learned to trust my fear. Demons don't spook easily, and most men don't scare me, but something about those two guys has me running downstairs as fast as I can go. When I reach the lobby, I run out of stairs and have to go out in the open. The path to the service elevator that takes me to the subbasement is blocked by a large group of people that seem to be arguing with the main desk staff. I have to get out of the building. Those men are there for me. I know they are. So I do the only reasonable thing—I run out the front door.

The hospital is in the middle of the city, so I don't have to run far before I'm on the street and mixed in with commuters. I force myself to slow to a walk and look around. I don't know Baltimore well, and the van I've been transported in doesn't have windows in the back, so I have no idea where I am or where to go. Worried about being on the street, I step into a crowded restaurant and look out the window. I can't even order a coffee and sit down. I've got no cash, no phone, no ID except the hospital badge, nothing. Crazy ideas start to fly through my mind. Can I wait until dark, go full demon, and run home? How long would that take? But if I go back to Northern Virginia, I'll have to deal with Ian. Maybe I should go up to Pennsylvania and hang out in the Poconos and eat sleeping campers. Now that I know I don't need to have sex with the guys, I wouldn't have to have different clothes to attract men. I could just go full demon and let go of my humanity. Except I don't want to do that. I don't want to live in the woods like the Pennsylvania version of the Jersey Devil. I'm on the verge of tears, so rather than draw attention to myself by burning holes in my clothes and the floor, I step back outside and continue walking away from the hospital. I'm not even sure what direction I'm going. I just keep walking.

I don't have a watch, so I'm not sure how long it took, but eventually, one of the white vans pulls ahead of me and parks on the side of the road. Bay Rum gets out and walks toward me. He stops about ten feet away. "Alma?"

I stop and stare at him. I don't know what to do.

"I know you're scared," he says. "But you don't have to be. Just get in the van. I'll take you someplace safe."

"Where?"

"A safe house in the mountains."

Is he serious? How weird is that? I wonder if it's actually in the Poconos.

"There are lots of trees. You'll like it."

"And if I don't?"

"Christ, Alma. Just get in the van. No one needs to die here."

I weigh my options, realize I don't have any good ones, and get in the van. Bay Rum sighs with relief as he follows me, closing the doors behind him.

Chapter 28: Going Down, Down, Down

The safe house is not in the Poconos, or we would've been there already. I've always had a good sense of time, so I estimate it's about six hours before the van stops. When Goldy opens the back door, and Bay Rum, Axe, and I get out, it looks like we're somewhere in the Appalachians—West Virginia or maybe western Virginia. Somewhere in coal country, anyway. The "safe house" is less of a house and more of an abandoned coal-processing plant. Great. The promised trees are there, but they're small and scrubby, a side effect of strip mining.

"Let's go," Bay Rum says and starts for one of three towering silos.

I know next to nothing about coal mining. In fact, were it not for the rusting sign designating the site as a processing plant, I wouldn't have guessed its purpose. I have no idea what the silos were originally built for. Coal, I guess, but as we walk around to the far side, away from the road, there is a small door at the bottom of one of the silos. Axe lifts a rusty panel to reveal a new-looking keypad. He types in a code and leans forward for a scan, either of his eye or his face. There's a series of loud clicks, and he opens the door and steps aside.

Is this my new prison?

"Go ahead," Bay Rum says.

I enter, and the guys follow, closing the door behind us. The interior is a surprise. It's a regular square room with twelve-foot ceilings and an elevator across from the door. Mounted on the wall next to the door is a large monitor with a small keyboard on a stand underneath. Next to the monitor is an old-school wall phone. Otherwise, it's a featureless room, white walls, white ceiling, no décor, no furnishings.

I turn to Bay Rum. "Seriously?"

"Sorry, Alma. It wasn't my call." He pushes the elevator button. The car is already there.

Sighing, I get in. The ride down isn't as long as it is at the hospital, but the car feels like it's going faster, so I'm guessing we're going pretty deep. When the car finally stops and the doors open, I'm surprised again. Instead of a dark hole like you see in the movies, it looks more like a bunker that you see in different sorts of movies. Unlike the hospital, the facility definitely feels like it's only for emergencies. The space is cramped. There are bunks and a card table with four chairs next to a kitchenette. Bay Rum leads me past all that to a separate room. "You'll be staying in here."

I look around him at the bunks. "You guys are going to be sleeping out there?"

"In shifts, yeah."

"How long do we have to stay here?"

"Until the boss calls the all clear."

"When's that going to be?"

Bay Rum shakes his head and sighs. "I don't know, Alma. I've never had to do this before."

I go into the small room. I guess it was designed for whoever was supposed to be in charge. It has a single bed and a small desk with a monitor on top and a keyboard, but whatever they're connected to seems to be inside the wall.

The room is half the size of my room back at the hospital, and the ceilings are only eight feet high. I hate it. When I'm in demon form, the room will feel even smaller. To my surprise, Bay Rum follows me into the room and closes the door behind us.

He sighs. "I suppose you've noticed there isn't a lock on the door."

I hadn't yet, but I would have. "Yeah."

"I would like it very much if you would stay in here."

I smile at him. "Why can't I just hang out with you guys? I'm not going to hurt anyone." Even as I say it, though, my demon stomach clenches inside me. I didn't get to eat earlier, and I've gotten used to regular meals. Maybe I should stay in here.

"It's not a good idea to let the guys get too comfortable around you."

"You seem pretty comfortable."

He sighs again and rubs his head. "Yeah, which might be very stupid of me. Look, no one wants to shoot you again. We don't know the ramifications of repeated exposure to that gun, and we shot you the night we captured you. So let's not do that again."

"Agreed. But I'm going to have to eat in the next day or so, or you're not going to have to shoot me."

He nods. "I know. We'll figure something out."

"Thanks."

He leaves, closing the useless door behind him. I stare at it for a few moments, thinking over my options. It's tight in this place. Those big guns aren't going to be easy to maneuver. There are only three of them, and I'm a lot stronger than I used to be. I could probably get out of here, but then what? Maybe I do have Stockholm syndrome, but I'm curious about my situation, and like it or not, Sefu and Peter are the only people I've met that are investigating demons. I have questions, and they seem to be the most likely to answer them. I'd like to get my soul back without having to kill thousands more men, and if I have any hope of that, I really need to keep my horse hooked to this cart. On the other hand, I'm already hungry. Shit.

I look around at the small room. Bored, I inspect the monitor on top of the desk. A wire runs from the monitor directly into the wall. I flick the on switch, hoping for an internet connection. No such luck. It looks like a closed-circuit video feed of the processing plant. That's it for entertainment, just rotating images of an abandoned coal plant. I open all the drawers in the desk. There's nothing in them, not even office supplies. I wonder if anyone has ever actually used this place. It seems relatively new; I doubt it's been here more than five years.

The single bed has a cheap polyester comforter on it, but when I pull it back, there aren't any sheets. There are two other doors in the room. I open one, and it's a closet. A plastic bag of sheets and a pillow are on the top shelf, but it's otherwise empty. I toss the plastic bag on the bed and open the other door. It's a small bathroom with a shower stall, a toilet, and a sink. There's a mirrored medicine cabinet over the sink, but it's empty. The whole facility looks like it was built from materials and fittings that could be found at any big-box home store. With nothing else to do, I make the bed and sit down on it. It's hard to imagine, but this place is so bleak it makes me miss my old cell. I wish I had something to read. I lie back on the bed and stare at the ceiling and realize there is a vent like the one in my cell back at the hospital. I can hear the fan whirring. I assume they're scrubbing the air here like they do at the hospital, which would explain the lack of dust.

I hear one of the guys laugh. Screw this. I get up and open the door. Two of them are sitting at the small table, playing cards. They stand, and Axe reaches for one of the big guns. Bay Rum holds up a palm at him.

"What do you need, Alma?"

"There's nothing to do in there." I take a seat at the table. "What are you guys doing?"

Axe lowers the gun and looks at Bay Rum.

"Where's Goldy?" I ask.

"Who?" Axe asks.

"Goldy, short for Gold Bond powder. You guys won't tell me your names, so I refer to you by your scents."

"He's upstairs on watch," Bay Rum says.

"Why? There's a monitor in my room. There's nothing out there."

"We need to make sure it stays that way," Bay Rum says.

"What do you call me, then?" Axe asks.

Bay Rum frowns at him.

"Axe."

Axe points at Bay Rum. "And him?"

"Bay Rum."

Bay Rum snorts at that. "You need to go back to your room, Alma."

"I don't want to. There's nothing to do in there. I'm bored."

"We're bored, too, but we're not complaining," Bay Rum says.

"You've got cards and company. I don't have anything, and that room is so small." I lean forward and put my elbows on the table. "Come on. Deal me in. I'm not going to hurt anyone."

Bay Rum rubs the back of his head, clearly trying to decide what to do with me. "Yeah, all right, but don't touch anyone."

"I wouldn't do that," I say, and I mean it.

They both sit back down, and Axe starts to shuffle the deck. "Do you know how to play gin rummy?"

"Yeah, I used to play with my dad."

Axe looks surprised. "Really?"

"What? Who taught you to play?"

"My roommate at the academy. I didn't realize you had a father."

"Everyone has a father."

"Sorry, I guess I thought you were spawned or something."

Bay Rum kicks him under the table.

"It's okay," I say. "I guess that's fair, but no, I'm not like a frog. I grew up in a regular house with regular parents."

"So how did you—"

Bay Rum kicks him again.

"Ow! Why can't I ask her questions?"

"No fraternization with the succubus," Bay Rum says.

"You were the one who said she could play cards with us!"

"Which was clearly a mistake. Alma, go back to your room."

"Come on! I'm not hurting anyone. Why can't we have a conversation? Just talking to me doesn't do anything."

Bay Rum rubs his cheek, clearly conflicted. I'm starting to wonder if it's not safe for them to discharge those big guns in here. Maybe I'm not as trapped as I thought.

"Yeah, okay," he says. "But no more questions." He glares at Axe.

"Fine," I say and happily shuffle the deck.

It's hard to tell time down in a hole, but we play cards, mostly gin rummy and some poker, for hours. Eventually, Bay Rum tells Axe to make dinner, which consists of boiling water to reconstitute freeze-dried meals. Nothing to write home about, but at least they're edible and make me feel slightly better. But I'm worried about needing to fill my soul stomach. I'm starting to ache, and distracting myself with cards isn't going to work much longer. After dinner, Axe goes up to watch, and Goldy comes down to eat. A few minutes later, the intercom squawks. I hadn't noticed the speaker on the wall by the door to the extra room before.

"We got a problem," Axe says.

Bay Rum presses the button to talk. "What kind of problem?"

"People."

"Go out and play security guard. Tell them they're trespassing."

"I don't think you understand. It's not one or two guys. It's a bus full of people. Look."

"A bus?" Bay Rum says and sticks his head in the other room to check the monitors. Goldy and I go in to look at them.

I laugh.

Bay Rum glares at me. "What's funny?"

"That's a party bus. I think you guys are about to host a rave."

"You've gotta be fucking kidding me," Bay Rum says. He presses the button on the intercom again. "Are they trying to get into the building?"

"No. They seem to be just setting up sound equipment outside. I got more people arriving, though."

"Okay. Just keep watch, and keep me posted if anything changes." He lets go of the intercom and shakes his head at Goldy and me. "What the hell?"

I shrug. "Kids."

"Idiots," Goldy says. "It's too dangerous to party in this place. Who knows what kind of chemicals are in the soil?"

"Not to mention all the rusted-out equipment," Bay Rum says grimly.

"You guys must have been loads of fun in college."

"I went into the army instead of college," Goldy says.

Bay Rum just frowns at me. "This is a mess."

My soul stomach takes that moment to remind me that I was supposed to eat hours ago. I look at the monitors and consider all the drunken, drugged-up guys that will soon be circulating above us. I don't say anything, though, and we return to the table and continue playing cards—with a distinct lack of enthusiasm. I'm bored, and they're concerned about the rave.

Time crawls by with Axe checking in every half hour. Every time we finish a round of cards, Bay Rum checks the monitors. He estimates about two hundred people at the party.

Eventually, Goldy yawns. "If you don't mind," he says to Bay Rum, "I'm going to hit the rack."

"Go ahead. I'm going to relieve Axe, and he can do the same. Alma, you're with me."

It amuses me that he's decided to run with the nicknames I've given them. I'm actually excited to go. How pathetic is that? But it's dead boring down here, and I'm sick of playing cards.

Chapter 29: The Lesser of Two Evils

We take the elevator up. Axe is looking at the monitor when the elevator doors open. He turns to look at us.

"Hit the rack," Bay Rum tells him. "I'll take it from here."

Axe looks confused. "She's staying with you?"

"You want to sleep with her downstairs?"

Axe looks away, embarrassed. "Point taken."

He leaves, and Bay Rum and I look at the monitor. "Looks like a happening party," I say.

Bay Rum just grunts at me and taps on the keyboard, and the monitor shifts to another camera.

The party really does look fun. Colored lights are bouncing off the silos and the processing plant. The throbbing music is so loud we can hear a muffled bit of it in here. The crowd is moving to the music, like one living organism undulating to the rhythm. People wearing glow-stick necklaces make the dancing crowd look like some kind of phosphorescent deep-sea creature. I have a strong desire to be out there and not just because I love a good party. This kind of scene is a great place to hunt. I consider suggesting that Bay Rum let me do my thing so I don't starve to death before Sefu calls, but I'm hesitant. He just keeps watching the monitor, where he can see all the camera feeds at once. I sit across the room and watch. With my demon-enhanced eyesight, I can see everything on the screens—even from way over here. I don't know exactly what time it is, but based on my internal clock and the movements of the crowd, I know it's around midnight.

We wait in silence, and I can't help wondering if he might be thinking the same thing I am—that I've got to eat, and this could be the perfect opportunity. Eventually, he sits down on the floor across from me.

Emboldened, I say, "You know, this could solve our problem."

He shakes his head. "I can't let you out there to kill someone."

"You take me to kill people all the time."

"Those are old men about to die anyway. This is different. Those are just kids out there."

My experience is that every big party has at least one predator, and I'm not talking about me. "Come on," I say. "They're the same age I am, and I assure you there is at least one asshole in that crowd who's trying to roofie some unsuspecting girl. What if I just take him out? We'd be doing the world a favor."

Bay Rum looks at me. "Seriously?"

"Yeah, I try not to kill good guys. They're in short enough supply as it is."

He gives me the side-eye.

"I need to eat, man. And I'm pretty sure keeping me alive is a high priority. So unless you're willing to sacrifice Goldy or Axe, we need to do something."

Bay Rum rubs his brow. "Christ." He stands and walks over to the monitor and peers at it closely. After a couple of minutes, one of the cameras goes close-up on an old guy tapping a keg. "What about this guy?"

I look at the old man. His skin is tanned from working in the sun, and the muscles in his arms are corded like he's done manual labor all his life. He smiles at a younger man, who brings him another keg and takes the one he just tapped. He's missing a few teeth.

"Surely, he's the best choice," Bay Rum says.

"You don't know that. What if this job is the only thing feeding his grandkids?"

"Come on, Alma."

"What? You don't know his life."

"But you can pick a predator out of a crowd of two hundred?" He frowns at me in disbelief.

"Every time," I say. "They're super easy to spot. They don't participate, don't drink much, don't do drugs at the party. Why? Because they're scanning, looking for prey, trying to spot someone vulnerable who's on their own or that they can easily separate from the herd."

"You sound like a National Geographic special."

"You'd be surprised how much of that stuff is the same in humans, especially bad ones."

He rubs his head. "I don't know, Alma. I can't just let you out to run amok."

"Run amok? What do you think I'm going to do, go berserk and kill a dozen guys?"

He looks at me like that's exactly what he thinks.

"I don't do that. I don't kill more than I need. I do a surgical strike for survival. That's it," I say, exasperated. "I don't know why you're being so squeamish. You let me loose on the hospital wards all the time."

"That's different."

"Yeah? You keep telling yourself that. Meanwhile, what are our options? You going to send Goldy and Axe out to collect someone for me? I hope whatever insurance plan Sefu provides includes therapy for you guys, because they're really going to need it after that."

He blows out a frustrated breath. "Fuck."

"No need. A kiss will do."

"That's not funny," he says grimly.

"No kidding," I reply, matching his tone.

"What would you do with the body?"

"The same thing I always do."

"Which is?"

"Leave it."

He shakes his head.

"If I try to hide it and it's found, then it looks like murder, and there's an investigation. If I leave it, then the guy died of a heart attack at an illegal rave. Not exactly unheard of."

He grits his teeth, the muscles in his jaw working. He's struggling with this decision, but the more we talk, the more he realizes this is the best option. All during the conversation, he's been glancing at the phone. I'd thought he was looking at the monitor, but now I think he's hoping Sefu will call and tell us to come back—so he won't have to decide.

Another hour passes, and the crowd on the monitor is starting to get sloppy as the booze and the drugs really take hold. People are starting to drift away to take their out-of-control friends home or to look for some privacy to hook up. Now is the time.

"Let me out. Oh, but first, do you have any cash?"

Bay Rum grits his teeth but gets out his wallet and hands me three twenties. He lays his palm on the door control panel and leans forward so it can scan him. When the door slides open, he says, "Don't make me regret this."

I flash him a grin. "No promises." I wink, and I'm through the door.

I'm still wearing the clothes of a hospital worker, so I decide to run with the idea of looking to get loose after work with no time to change. I come around the side of the silo to where the party is like I've just arrived. I've already picked my target from the security camera feeds. He's wearing tight jeans, shiny black cowboy boots, and a black button-down shirt. He's hovering near the makeshift bar, looking for his own target. I go up to the end of the bar nearest him and order three shots of Fireball. The bartender doesn't even raise an eyebrow. He just pours my shots, takes my cash, and moves on to the next guy.

I down my first shot and note that my target is watching. Good, that was the point. I finish off the other two with ease and no discernible reaction. Alcohol doesn't seem to affect me anymore.

I take a deep breath and mutter to myself like I'm trying to psych myself up, then I head for the dance floor and sway awkwardly at the edge of the crowd near my mark so he can see how hard I'm trying to be confident. So he can read me as insecure and a little desperate. Sure enough, after a few minutes, he saunters up and starts dancing near me. Pretty soon, he's dancing with me. Eventually, he leans over and asks if he can buy me a drink, and I agree. We go back to the bar, and he starts making conversation while we wait for the bartender to notice us.

"You look like you just came from work," he shouts over the music. He doesn't have a West Virginia accent.

I tug at my scrub top like I'm embarrassed. "I know," I shout back, upping the Southern accent in my own voice. "I had to work late, and I didn't want to miss the party by going home to change. I live way up on the mountain, so it would've taken forever to go home first."

"Are you a nurse?"

"Tech," I say. He doesn't bother asking what kind. He was trying to assess my education level, not get to know me.

"Cool." He looks around. "Kind of a crazy place for a party."

I shrug. "These guys do them wherever they can find a spot."

"This is my first one. Do you go a lot?"

I shrug again. "If they're close and I'm not working."

"I'm Pete."

"Mary," I lie, but that's okay. He's lying too. I can smell it.

The bartender shows up, and the guy orders two more shots of Fireball. Good, he was paying attention.

We return to the dance floor, and this time, he's dancing much closer, rubbing up against me. He vacillates between aggressive and flirty, always backing up when I react like he's pushing it, but then he'll push again. We return to the bar and then back to the dance floor a few more times. I let him push. I wish it wasn't taking so long. I'm conscious of the fact that Bay Rum is watching. I don't like it. Hunting is a private thing, not something for show. I feel like he's behind that monitor taking notes so he can report back to Sefu: *Subject lures men with Fireball and bad dancing.*

Finally, Pete asks me if I want to go somewhere more private. I agree. He goes back to the bar and brings back a couple of beers and hands me one. And there it is, the bitter flavor of roofies. He chose an IPA in an attempt to hide the drug, but you can't hide drugs from a demon's tongue. You can't drug a demon either. I drink the adulterated beer as I follow him back to his car, which is parked in the far back corner of the lot, away from the lights of the party. I'm self-conscious because Bay Rum's watching, so when Pete opens the driver's-side door and hits the button to unlock the passenger side, I don't bother walking around and instead step in for a kiss. This surprises him, but he rolls with it, which is his first and last mistake.

I suck out his little soul and hold him up by his shirt. I am definitely stronger than I used to be because slipping him into the driver's seat is really easy. I feel around his pockets and find a little vial of cocaine and a plastic baggie of roofies. Perfect. I smear some coke under his nose, sprinkle a little on his shirt, and dump the rest in his mouth under his tongue. I close the car door and look around. The music is still pounding, but more people are starting to leave. I consider running, but I don't know where I am exactly—or where I'd run to even if I knew. Resigned, I keep to the shadows, skirting the perimeter of the party back to the silo. When I approach the door, it slides open, and a grim-faced Bay Rum is waiting for me on the other side. I step in, and he palms the door closed behind me. He stares at me with his jaw clenched.

"What?"

He shakes his head and walks to the other side of the room. "Nothing."

I sigh and sit down on the floor with my back against the wall. Would it kill them to have a couch or a couple of chairs up here?

Bay Rum sits across from me and stares at the floor. His silence is annoying. Pete's tiny soul is flopping around inside me, barely a snack.

I've gotten used to the nice big souls of the dying men in the hospital. Bay Rum looks at the monitor, watching the party winding down. It's after three, and everyone who has to work later today is already gone.

The intercom next to the wall squawks, and Bay Rum stands up to answer it. Axe asks if he wants relief, but Bay Rum declines and sits back down.

He shakes his head at me. "Doesn't it even bother you that you killed that guy in cold blood?"

"Nope. He was an asshole. He roofied me—or tried to. That stuff doesn't work on me anymore. Taking him out of the gene pool was a gift to society."

"But you don't know anything about him."

"I know he preyed on women. Not just me and not just once. He was a monster just like I am. When I kill other monsters, I see it as fair play."

He sighs. "Fuck, Alma. You murdered him, and I aided and abetted. That's not supposed to bother me?"

I roll my eyes. "You opened a door. If that's aiding and abetting, every doorman in the country is culpable of something. Let it go."

He shakes his head again. "This fucking job."

I feel bad for the guy. I really do. Neither of us wants to be where we are. "How is this all that different from what we do at the hospital?"

"You think I'm okay with what we do at the hospital? Because I'm not."

"Good."

He raises his eyebrows in confusion. "What?"

"I'm glad you're not okay with it. That tells me you're a good person in a bad situation, which, believe it or not, is exactly what I am."

He frowns. "You may look like a person, but I know you're not one."

"But I used to be. None of this was my choice. I wasn't born this way. I want to be the woman I once was."

"How did you get like this?"

"I met a guy on campus. We hung out, and he was sweet and fun and really smart. We dated for a while, and then we slept together—and I woke up like this."

He snorts. "That sounds like some kind of horror movie shit. Casual sex makes you a monster."

"I don't know how casual it was. We were in a committed relationship. I loved him. I thought he loved me too. But he was an incubus just looking to expand his harem."

"Harem?"

I shrug. "Yeah, it's a thing. If I wanted to keep being a demon, apparently, I could do the same thing to guys."

"How?"

"I don't know. I don't know how any of this works. In demon terms, I'm practically an infant."

"You don't look like an infant. You're bigger than I am."

I sigh. "I know, but that doesn't change the fact that I know very little about being a demon."

"You know how to kill."

"I know how to feed myself, but Ian had to tell me what to do. Of course, he lied and made it way more complicated than it actually is, which I assume he did just to amuse himself."

"Sounds like a real charmer."

"He was once. But you saw him as he really is. Fun guy, right?"

"So that thing that attacked us that night in the alley turned you into a demon?"

"Yep. Thus, forever altering my life and yours."

"What an asshole."

I can't help chuckling at that. "Right?"

Chapter 30: Fresh Air

Silence falls between us, and I go back to watching the party fall apart on the monitors. Eventually, the guys working the party start to break down the makeshift bar, which is the real end of any party. Pretty soon, there's nothing left to look at but a few bits of trash blowing around and not even much of that. For an illegal rave, they've been pretty tidy.

"I guess that's it, then."

Bay Rum looks at me. "I guess so."

Part of me wants to engage in chitchat, ask him about where he grew up, where he went to school, but I'm pretty sure he wouldn't tell me. He's sitting against the wall, looking up at the ceiling. His face is still, but anxiety is radiating off of him. Like a good soldier, he can hide his fears—just not from me. My nose reads him like he was telling me his troubles out loud.

I can hear the elevator coming up the shaft. He must hear it, too, because he gets to his feet and seems to pull himself together, shifting into boss mode. When the elevator opens, Goldy gets out. He looks freshly showered, but his clothes are still rumpled from yesterday.

Bay Rum nods to him and turns to me. "Let's go."

I follow him onto the elevator, impressed by how smoothly they work as a team.

When the doors close, he says, "When we get downstairs, I want you to go into the room and close the door. Get some sleep. I'm going to take a shower and hit the rack. Axe will be up and sitting guard, so don't give him any reason to be nervous."

"No problem." I'm tired enough to sleep. "It's mind-numbing in this place. Sleep would be a welcome relief."

When the elevator doors open again, the smell of breakfast food is in the air. Axe is sitting at the table eating, and he points at two bags on the counter.

"Want breakfast? It's biscuits and gravy. Not bad. Kettle's already hot."

Bay Rum looks at me. "Sit down."

I sit at the table while he makes the meals. I don't know that I'd describe the food as good, but it's surprisingly edible, if not plentiful. I really wish the scumbag's soul had been bigger. It's not going to be long before I need to eat again, and the likelihood of another rave is pretty slim.

"Okay." Bay Rum stands and puts his breakfast bag in the trash.

I do the same and then retreat to the other room unprompted. I get undressed and get into bed, but instead of sleeping, I stare at the ceiling tiles and listen.

The place is so small I can hear the shower running and then the bed creaking when I assume Bay Rum lies down.

I don't remember going to sleep, but at some point, I must have, because the sound of people moving around in the outer room wakes me. Without thinking, I stand up and bang my head on the eight-foot ceiling. My demon form is definitely getting bigger. I quickly resume my human form and get dressed. I open the door just a crack and ask, "Hey, can I come out now?"

Goldy and Bay Rum are sitting at the table eating.

"Yeah," Bay Rum says. "Water's hot. Make yourself something to eat."

I look through the cabinet, which is stocked with bag after bag of dehydrated food. I settle on a bag that says it's maple sugar oatmeal with walnuts. I turn back to the guys and hold it up. "Is this one any good?"

Goldy nods. "Yeah, if you like those little packets from the grocery store."

Those little packets were a staple of my childhood, so it sounds good to me. I fill the bag of oatmeal with hot water. The coffeepot is half-full, so I pour myself a cup and sit at the table. My soul stomach reminds me that last night's soul was paltry. I don't want to talk about my needs in front of Goldy, though. Bay Rum seems to want to shield the other two from what happened yesterday, and I'm happy to comply. The fewer people having personal crises over what I am, the better.

The guys are starting to smell a little ripe. Even though they're showering, there's no laundry room here, so their clothes are starting to be the worse for wear. I wonder how much longer we're going to have to be down in this hole.

Goldy finishes eating and puts his bag in the trash.

"Go up and talk to Axe," Bay Rum says. "I want you two to come up with a supply plan. We're going to need food, more water, and some fresh clothes."

Goldy nods and heads for the elevator.

When the doors close behind Goldy, Bay Rum looks at me. "I don't know how much longer we're going to have to be here, so I think we better talk about feeding you."

"Yeah, that's going to need to happen sooner than I'd hoped. That guy's soul was pathetic."

Bay Rum's jaw twitches. "Great."

The phone rings, and Bay Rum stands to pick up the receiver. "Right. Understood." He hangs up and turns to me. "We're done here."

I sigh with relief. "Thank goodness."

"I doubt goodness has anything to do with it."

He hits the intercom button and tells the guys to come down and gather their gear, which takes less time than their ride down in the elevator. Goldy takes the trash bag out of the can, Bay Rum does a last sweep, and then we all pile into the elevator. I can feel relief coming off Goldy and Axe, but Bay Rum is still on high alert.

Goldy throws the trash bag into the back of the van, and he and I clamber in after it. Axe gets behind the wheel, Bay Rum takes the passenger seat, and we're on our way back to Baltimore. I lean forward in my seat so I can see out the windshield. West Virginia has provided us with a beautiful sunny day, and the trees and the mountains are especially vibrant. I don't know if it's really that good or if I've just spent too much time underground and indoors, but I don't care. I'm enjoying the natural beauty around me while I have the chance.

Unfortunately, we're out of the country and into suburban sprawl long before I'm ready. I sit back and wonder what went on at the hospital while we were gone. I wonder who those two men from the helicopter were and whether anyone is going to tell me. I wonder what Sefu and Peter will have to say about my running out of the hospital and whether there will be repercussions for that. For the briefest of seconds, I consider going full demon, ripping the doors off the van, and running into the night. But, like always, I can't see the next step after escaping. My circumstances are limited less by the guards and more by inexperience—not just as a demon but as an adult. I'm so out of my depth, and I hate it. I wish I could talk to Mom, but it's not like she can give me useful information she learned growing up as a demon. I can feel myself getting upset, so I blow out a calming breath and try to keep from crying. Putting holes in the floor of the van with acid tears isn't likely to endear me to the guys, and my life is better if they like me.

Axe and Goldy have been chatty since we left the coal-processing plant. Mostly, they talk about wanting to go home, take showers, sleep in their own beds, and eat real food—that kind of stuff. Bay Rum has said nothing, and his silence has me worried. Clearly, this little outing was more succubus time than he bargained for. I can't help wondering if people who work on super-top-secret projects are allowed to quit and, if they are, how long they're allowed to live afterward. I hope Bay Rum isn't going to do anything rash. And if he does, I hope Sefu isn't going to expect me to handle it.

Chapter 31: Fallout

When we arrive back at the hospital, Axe pulls the van into the underground garage and onto a freight elevator that takes us farther underground than the garage goes. When we get out of the van, Sefu is waiting. He looks tired and a little rumpled.

"Stow your gear," he says to the guys. "Debriefing in the conference room in five."

The guys nod their understanding and head off together. I assume they have a locker room or something like it, but I've never seen it—or a conference room, for that matter.

Sefu looks at me. "You ran off."

"Those two men terrified me. I had to get out of here."

Sefu nods like what I just said makes total sense. "Quite right. Your instincts were spot-on. Those were very dangerous men."

"Who were they?"

"Members of a rival organization with different goals regarding your kind."

"What does that mean?" Sefu once said he worked for an organization called SEU, which stands for Seeking the Elegant Universe, but he's never said explicitly what their goals were.

He shakes his head. "I don't have time to get into all that now. I assume you're hungry."

I'm guessing he doesn't know about last night, but it doesn't matter, because that guy's soul is already fading. "I am."

"Go back to your room. The meal you missed is still in a persistent vegetative state. Someone will fetch you soon."

"All right, then." But he's already walking away.

Apparently, my rapid departure didn't upset him, so I walk back to my room on my own. There are still hazmat-suited guards in the hallways, but none of them seem too bothered about my movements. As I pass Peter's lab, Jerry steps out. I almost run into him.

"Hey."

"Hi, Cupcake."

He looks healthier than the last time I saw him. His cheeks have more color, and he looks like he's put on a few pounds. His clothes fit instead of hanging off him.

"What are you doing here?"

He actually smiles. "Just some tests for Father Peter."

"What happened to him being the enemy?"

He shrugs. "Your enemy, Cupcake. I'm not a demon anymore."

"So you're just letting them poke and prod you out of the goodness of your heart?"

"Of course not. I haven't had any health care since I got my soul back. They've done blood work and tissue samples and given me a full physical and hearing and eye tests—stuff I need." He reaches into the pocket of his shirt and pulls out a pair of glasses. "Really need."

"Well, that's great, Jerry." I wish I had my soul back. "What do they get out of it?"

He shrugs. "They don't talk about that, but my guess is to compare my samples to yours."

I can't help but snort at that.

"What?"

"They couldn't get any samples from me. No blood, no tissue."

Jerry looks confused. "That's weird."

"Right? They did test my eyes and hearing and how fast I could run and stuff like that."

I notice that there are two more hazmat guards in the hall now. I wonder if maybe Jerry and I aren't supposed to be talking or if they're just not sure whether we're supposed to be talking. The body language of the guards reads as uncertainty.

"I haven't done the running test yet. That's scheduled for tomorrow. Father Peter had to leave early today."

"Yeah? Why's that?"

Jerry shrugs again. "Who knows? They're not exactly forthcoming around here."

"Then why work with them?"

"Because that African guy told me he'd get new credentials for me, and he's already come through with a driver's license. Do you know how hard it is to do stuff without a valid ID?"

"How'd you get the job at the hotel, then?"

"Ian got me that job. He knows the owner. He knows everybody. He's got multiple personas, and they all have ID—which isn't a problem for someone with all that money."

"Ian's rich?"

Jerry raises his eyebrows in surprise. "Are you kidding?"

"What? I know he has money, but I always thought it was, like, drug-dealer money, not rich-guy money."

Jerry shakes his head like I'm an idiot, and I'm starting to feel like one.

"Well, you're kind of right. He does have friends in low places. But also, Ian's been alive for a really long time. He belongs to several clubs, the old-money kind. He's got all kinds of money."

"I never saw any of his fancy personas, only the mean, crappy kind."

"Because you're still a baby demon. As time goes by, you'll see all kinds of things." He looks at his phone. "I need to go. I'll see you around."

"Yeah, okay."

He heads for the elevators, and I go back to my room to ruminate on what he's said.

When I open the door, I notice they've given me some new DVDs and books. I'm a little appalled by how happy I am to be back in this room with its high ceilings and entertainment options. I take a shower and settle onto the bed to read an old thriller by a Ross Macdonald. The paperback is dry and brittle, but the story is pretty good.

A little while later, a hazmat goon I don't recognize knocks on the door and tells me to get dressed for upstairs. He doesn't specify who I should be, so I pick one of the IDs I already have and get dressed to go collect trash and a soul.

Minutes later, I'm walking by the window with the view of the helipad, which is empty today. I stop for a moment and look at it. I wish someone would tell me who those men were, who they work for, and how exactly they rival Sefu and Peter. My soul stomach reminds me of the task at hand, and I walk down the hall to find a much younger man than I'm used to seeing. I take a quick peek at his chart and find that he's been in a motorcycle accident. Massive head trauma. I barely have to kiss him, and his soul slips into my mouth like it's been waiting for me. I try not to be sad about his situation as I push my trash cart back toward the elevators. The alert is still going off at the nurses' station as the elevator doors close behind me.

I'm surprised when I get back to my room that the phone is ringing. I pick up the heavy receiver. "Hello?"

"Cup..." a voice gasps. "Cupcake?"

"Jerry?"

Chapter 32: Crisis Management

Jerry doesn't respond, and I can feel panic bubbling up. It's not like I love the guy, but there aren't many people in the world who truly understand what I'm going through.

"Hey! Jerry!" Still nothing.

I put the receiver on the dresser and go to open the door to shout for someone in the hall, but it's locked. I pound on the door. "Hey! Hey! I need some help in here!"

No one comes to the door. I pick up the receiver again, but the connection is gone, and all I hear is a dial tone. I hang up and return to the door, stripping off my clothes. In demon form, I pound on the door and shout in a full-throated howl. They may not open the door, but at least they won't be able to ignore me. The phone rings behind me.

I rush over and pick up the receiver, or at least, I try to, but big claws aren't good for that. I transform, just my arm, back to human form and pick up. "Jerry?"

"Alma, it's me," Sefu says in a soothing voice. "Please calm down. I've already got a team routed to Jerry."

"You know where he is?"

"Of course. We've been tracking him with his phone and a tag on his car."

"How far out are they?" For once, I'm relieved this organization is so intrusive.

"The van was already in the city, so they should have him in the next couple of minutes."

"Do you know what happened?" I'm pacing the room. I eyeball the light at the top of the ceiling, where I'm sure they have a camera. I must look pretty ridiculous, a big pink demon with one dainty human arm.

"No. Assuming he needs medical attention, they will treat him in transit and bring him in through the emergency room." He sounds so calm I want to smack him.

"The guys can treat him?"

"Everyone on the team is an emergency medical technician."

"Okay." That makes me feel somewhat better.

He pauses like he's trying to decide something. "If that creature that came after you has gone after Jerry, would you be able to tell?"

I think about that for a second. Jerry smells weird but not like a demon. Ian's stench is profound. If Ian went after Jerry, he'd reek.

"Yes."

"Then pull yourself together and get dressed. Put on one of the waste-disposal badges—I don't care which one—and meet me at the elevator." He hangs up.

I do as he says, grabbing the first badge in the drawer. The photo is of a limp-haired, bottle-blond woman who looks to be around my age. I transform into her and quickly get dressed. I hear the locking mechanism open just as I reach for the door. Hazmat guys are in the hall, but they pay little attention to me as I head to the elevator. Sefu is already there. He has a badge around his neck that reads *Dr. Sefu Omandi*. Below that, in smaller print, is *Genetics* and below that *Research Fellow*, so now I know his name and his job.

"You're a doctor?"

He presses the button to call the elevator and nods at me.

"Impressive, but I thought you were a physicist."

"I am."

"Ooh, both kinds of doctor. Fancy."

He arches an eyebrow at me.

"Sorry. I babble when I'm worried."

He smiles. "Indeed. They're bringing Jerry in now."

The elevator arrives, and we step in.

When the doors open again, we're at the lobby, and I follow Sefu to the ER. When the automatic sliding doors open, it's immediately clear that Jerry is not okay. He's being wheeled in on a stretcher by big guys I don't recognize. They have blood on their arms and shirts. Jerry is covered in blood, and bandages cover his face and torso. His clothes are hanging off him in shreds. One of the guys is holding the bandage on Jerry's face while helping steer the stretcher with his other hand. Doctors and nurses are coming from all directions.

"Aren't you going to help?" I ask Sefu.

"I would be in the way. Emergency medicine is not my specialty. Can you tell what attacked him?"

I don't need my nose to tell me it was Ian. The scratches are clearly claw marks. I walk past the room where the staff is working hard to get the bleeding under control. A nurse rushes by me with two bags of blood. Jerry looks bad. He's clearly lost a lot of blood and is startlingly pale. I can smell Ian's stench from where I'm standing.

One of the doctors says, "What is this, a bear attack? Where did they find this guy?"

Sefu touches my shoulder. "Come. We can't do anything else here."

Reluctantly, I follow him back to the lobby and to the elevators. "Are they going to call the cops and tell them there's a bear loose in Baltimore?"

"Possibly." His face is still, giving the appearance of calm indifference, but I can smell anxiety on him. Sefu is worried.

I decide to press the issue. "So you're okay with the police wasting time and resources looking for a bear that doesn't exist?"

He sighs. "What would you have me do, Alma? Call them and tell them to look for a demon instead?"

I frown at him.

"Even if I did that, and by some miracle, they believed me, do you imagine the Baltimore police are equipped to deal with your big friend?"

"He's not my friend." Quite the opposite.

"Yes, well, either way, they can't deal with him. But we might be able to. I need to talk to Peter."

"Where is he?"

"Working on getting the second site ready, but he's on his way back."

"Second site? You're not thinking of moving to that hole in West Virginia?"

He smiles. "No. The coal plant is a safe house, not a research facility."

"So where's the research facility?"

"A couple hours north, in the mountains. It's more secure. I'd have you there now if we could sort out how to feed you. But the hospital is the best setting for that."

I'm shocked at his candor. Sefu has never answered my questions so directly before.

"Peter has suggested transferring you back and forth, but if that monster can track your scent, taking you in and out is a bad idea. Obviously, that's true, since he's now in Baltimore. The more we take you out of our scrubbed-air environment, the more he'll be able to zero in on your location. Clearly, he needs to be dealt with before we can transfer you anywhere."

"Why can't I stay here?" I can't believe I just said that, but lately, the outside world seems less and less safe.

"Because you are not the only one with enemies, and I can't hold mine at bay indefinitely. It was fine to do research here before you came along. Now it's too public."

The idea that his deep underground research facility is public seems laughable, but it is right in the middle of the city, which reminds me that Ian attacked Jerry in the middle of the city, in the daytime. I can't help wondering how he did that and why. What did he gain by going after Jerry? Was it just rage because he can't get his hands on me?

"After the team cleans up, I want you to sit in on the debriefing." The elevator doors open. "For now, go back to your room. I'll send for you when it's time."

"Okay." I walk back to my room, wondering how much blood a person can lose without dying.

Chapter 33: Debriefing

It feels like a long time, but finally, there's a knock on my door. I open it to find a hazmat goon, who escorts me past Sefu's office and down a hallway I've never been in before. All the hallways are white, so it's not easy to tell, but this one smells different. The commingled scents of several men tell me this is where the crew guarding me bunks, showers, and gathers for meals. We walk past a row of small lockers. They're too small for clothing, so I wonder if the guys have to surrender their cell phones when they come down here.

The goon with me stops and opens a door. Inside, Sefu is sitting at the head of a long table, with Peter on his right. At the opposite end of the table are three men whose faces I've never seen. I'm frankly surprised I'm seeing them now. No one is in a hazmat suit.

"Take a seat, Alma." Sefu points at the chair on his left. The men at the other end of the table shift, clearly uncomfortable with my presence. "These are the men who picked up Jerry."

"Thank you," I say to the three of them and mean it. It's important to me that Jerry survives. If Jerry can make it, maybe I can too.

Sefu clears his throat. "Start at the beginning," he says to the men. "Don't leave anything out."

The guy in the middle nods his head. "When we got the call that that we needed to pick up a target, we were at the Royal Farms on Keswick Road, gassing up the van. The tracker put him in Wyman Park, just off Carnegie Way near Olin Hall. We had him in the van in less than five minutes."

Sefu holds up a hand. "Slow down. When you arrived on scene, what did you see?"

"We parked in front of Olin Hall and went the rest of the way on foot. He was in the trees behind the building. It looked like he'd been dragged there, but he was bleeding so bad that we just loaded him and headed for the hospital."

"You didn't see anyone?"

"Just some students going in and out of the building but no one in the woods."

"Did you see any clothing on the ground?" Peter asks.

The guy in the middle looks at the other two, who shake their heads. "No."

Sefu sighs. "All right, then. Thank you for your efforts. Hopefully, he will pull through. I'll let you know either way."

"Thank you, sir," the guy in the middle says.

Sefu nods. "You're dismissed."

The three men leave, and it's just Sefu and Peter and me left in the room.

Peter shakes his head in frustration. "How could a creature that large attack Jerry in broad daylight without anyone noticing? Shouldn't there have been shreds of clothing on the scene from when he transformed? Surely, he didn't take the time to undress."

I can't help snorting at that.

"What?" Peter says.

I shake my head. "You're basing Ian's actions on mine. He's so much more advanced than I am. I don't think he ever wears actual clothes. When he transforms, everything is him—including his clothes."

"Would he even need to completely transform?" Sefu asks. "After all, earlier, you transformed just your arm so you could pick up the phone."

Peter raises his eyebrows at that.

"Presumably, he can do that too."

"I've never specifically seen him do that, but I'm certain he can."

"If you can transform into a clothed person, why don't you?" Peter asks.

"I can't. Or I can't yet, at least, not completely and not for very long. Holding form takes a lot of effort. The less I have to keep track of, the better. When you see me dressed, underneath my clothes isn't really defined like the parts of me you can see. If I had to form the clothes, too, I might screw up, so it's safer to just get dressed. But Ian is way more powerful than I am. He probably does it with ease."

Sefu strokes his goatee. "We need more information about him."

I sigh. So far, I've been reluctant to throw Ian to these guys because it would feel like betrayal. But now Ian's getting too close. I don't know what he wants from me, but it doesn't feel like anything good. Meanwhile, Sefu and Peter might be my only chance at getting my humanity back sooner rather than later.

"All I know is he's reputed to be very old and very rich, and he has a town house in Georgetown that's just one big three-story room with steel scaffolding inside to hold up the structure."

"You know where he lives, and you're just now divulging this?" Sefu says with clear irritation.

"Did you forget the part where you captured and imprisoned me?" I say, glaring at him.

He glares back.

"She has a point," Peter says, trying to defuse the situation. "Besides, that was then. This is now. What are we going to do about him?"

Sefu frowns at me and then turns to Peter. "We're going to start by getting surveillance teams on that town house. We need a mobile unit, too, in case he leaves. Movements, habits, associates, all of that is important information." He glares at me again. "Is there anything else you've been holding back?"

"I was supposed to meet him every day in an alley in Vienna to do a soul exchange. Other succubi met him there too."

I see the muscles in Sefu's jaw clench. "Fine, we'll get a team on that too. Anything else?"

I shrug. "Nope."

"Fine."

"Hey, am I going to do any more Krav Maga training?" I'm feeling kind of antsy, so it would be nice to burn off some of this nervous energy.

Sefu shakes his head. "Not here."

Again, without any obvious signal, the hazmat goon comes back in. I guess they're done with me, but Sefu surprises me.

"What is it?" he asks the goon.

"Phone call from upstairs."

"Ah," Sefu says, rising from his chair. "I will be back."

He follows the goon out, leaving me alone with Peter.

"So, Sefu tells me you've been setting up a new facility." I can tell from the surprise on Peter's face that he didn't know Sefu had told me.

He nods slowly. "Yes."

"But you guys don't know how to feed me there."

"It's a conundrum, yes."

I laugh. "A conundrum. Is that what it is?"

Before Peter can respond, the door opens.

Sefu steps inside and looks at me. "Jerry is awake and asking for you."

I follow him out to the elevators. "How is he?"

"He's suffered several serious lacerations and lost a lot of blood but no broken bones and no head trauma. As long as he can avoid sepsis, he should make a full recovery albeit with significant scarring. They've given him antibiotics and painkillers, so I don't know how coherent he will be, but he's agitated, and they feel like he might calm down if he can see you. He's told them you're his girlfriend."

"Great." I roll my eyes, but I don't really care. I'd like to see for myself how he's doing, because earlier, he looked like he was at death's door.

When we exit at the lobby, I follow Sefu to the intensive care unit. I'm shocked when I see Jerry. I'm not sure what I was expecting, but it wasn't this. Sefu goes to talk to Jerry's nurse while I stand at the foot of his bed. His head is rolling back and forth, and his eyes are clenched shut. He does seem agitated. While he's been cleaned up, none of his wounds are bandaged. They aren't bleeding, but they aren't stitched up either. I don't know how that works, but it's pretty horrifying to look at. At least his color is a little better. He stirs and opens his eyes, but it seems to take him a few moments to focus. I'm guessing they've got him on some pretty strong pain meds.

"Cupcake?" he says weakly.

It's clear he's trying not to move his mouth too much because the gash on his cheek looks like it goes all the way through. I'm not sure, but I think I can see his teeth. Maybe it's just the light, though. I hope it's the light.

"Cupcake?" he says again.

I don't really want to get any closer. It's really hard to look at him, but I move to the head of the bed so he can see me better.

"You gotta get me out of here," Jerry says plaintively. "He'll come back. He can be anybody. You're not safe either. We should both be downstairs."

"Okay," I say. "It's okay. I'll ask about moving you. You'll be safe."

His head lolls back, and he blinks slowly a few times before succumbing to the drugs and falling asleep.

Sefu comes back. "It's time to go."

I follow him back out to the elevators. "He's scared."

"I'm sure. I spoke to the nurse. She's going to have his doctor call me."

"We need to get him out of there. Ian can walk in as anyone and finish what he started."

He nods grimly. "I've got men all around the hospital, but I don't know how effective that is, since they don't know who they're looking for."

"Can't we bring him downstairs so the air scrubbers can mask his scent?"

"We'll see. I need to speak to his doctor. Trauma isn't my specialty, but I can tell you infection and sepsis are the fears right now. Ultimately, I'd like him at the second site, but for now, if we can bring him downstairs, that should be sufficient until we can move him."

I can't smell him, but I can feel Ian closing in. Jerry's state is proof of Ian's rage. Tension creeps up my spine and has all my senses on high alert. He's coming for me. I know it.

Chapter 34: The Best-Laid Plans

When the elevator doors open, Sefu uses his badge to access the subbasement levels. We begin the descent in silence, but I can't get the image of Jerry out of my mind.

"I don't understand why his wounds were all gaping like that but they weren't bleeding."

"I am sure they left them open because they still have debriding to do," he says without looking at me.

Debriding sounds nauseating. "I don't understand why he wasn't bleeding."

"Some of that is probably his own natural clotting, but I'm sure the doctors cauterized the larger bleeders."

"That sounds horrible."

"I assure you it was. When I was young, a woman in my village was attacked by a lion." He shook his head.

"She died?"

"No, but her recovery was grueling and her scars horrific. Jerry has a hard path with much pain ahead of him." He looks at me, his mouth a grim line. "In fact, given the layout of his wounds, it looks like that was the point."

"I don't understand."

"There was nothing random about his injuries. Nothing vital was hit. Each limb has exactly four deep slashes. The cut on his cheek is the most significant and deliberate. I think it was less that Jerry was attacked and more that he was tortured."

"Why would Ian torture him?"

Sefu raises an eyebrow at me. "Why indeed? The more I consider it, the more I think we need to get you and Jerry out of here as soon as possible. Tonight, even."

"I thought we couldn't move Jerry right now."

"It's not ideal, no, but given the danger, it might be the lesser of two evils."

"Well, out of any two evils, I assure you, Ian is always the worst one."

Sefu nods gravely. "I will call and let them know Jerry needs to be moved." The elevator stops and the doors open. "Go back to your room. Someone will come and collect you later."

"Okay."

I walk down the long white hall, passing hazmat goons at every intersection with other hallways. None of them seem familiar, and I can't smell them through their suits. They aren't standing like Bay Rum, Goldy, Axe, or Ocean. I wonder if those guys are off duty. Maybe Sefu gave Bay Rum, Goldy, and Axe some time off after West Virginia, or maybe they're all at the second site now. I know it's weird, but I kind of miss them.

In my room, I lie across the bed and stare at the ceiling. I feel anxious about Ian—and about moving to a second site where there won't be easy meals around. Though I don't regret killing the guy at the rave, since he was his own kind of monster, I don't miss hunting. Well, okay, I do kind of miss hunting. But only bad guys, and they aren't always around, and it's a lot of work, and it doesn't always go well, and it's not a very human thing to do.

I sit up and get undressed. When I'm naked, I drop my human form and look in the full-length mirror. I can easily reach over the top of the door now, although I can't reach the ceiling. My horns are definitely longer, a couple of inches at least. I guess I'm maturing as a demon, and I don't like it. I want to mature as a human. I think about my mother. I look a lot like her, and I always figured that I'd age the way she has. It doesn't look like that now. I think about Jerry and his gaping wounds and wonder if he regrets choosing to go back to being human. If he and Ian had gone head-to-head as demons, would the outcome have been different? I don't know, and I'm afraid to find out.

The phone rings. When I pick up the receiver, Sefu says, "Could you revert back to human form? I'm sending a bag over so you can pack your things."

I look around the room. What things? All that's in here are a bunch of old books and DVDs and some clothes that aren't mine. "Yeah, okay."

He hangs up, and I turn back into my old self. Sighing, I get dressed in scrubs. There's a knock on the door before it opens, so I know it isn't Sefu. Instead, a goon hands me a gym bag.

"The boss says to pack your clothes and IDs and anything else you want to take with you."

"Sure."

He closes the door again. I empty the drawers of clothes and hospital IDs before sorting through the books and DVDs. I stuff all the books I haven't read into the bag with the clothes. I decide to take the *Planet Earth* DVDs with me, even though I've seen them. Maybe I'll luck out, and the new site will have decent televisions. I'm guessing there's no hope for internet. Keeping that in mind, I pack all the DVDs, just in case no more are forthcoming. And since that might be true for books, too, I pack the rest of those. I get my toiletries out of the bathroom, and I'm done—my packing took a whopping five minutes. Assuming that I'll be leaving imminently, I start pacing around the room.

No one comes.

I pull an old Robert B. Parker novel out of my bag and lie down to read. I'm a quarter of the way through before Sefu opens the door and comes in. I sit up and yawn before stuffing the book back in the bag. "What time is it?"

Sefu looks at the gold watch on his wrist. "Almost two. Are you ready?"

I shrug. "For what?"

"We're going to the new site. I'm sending Jerry by ambulance. The rest of us will follow in the vans. Peter will bring up the rear with—I understand you call him Bay Rum."

I chuckle at that.

"The concern is obviously your big friend. At two o'clock in the morning, we should have minimal traffic around the hospital. The goal is to get out of the city as quickly and safely as possible."

"And if Ian does show up?"

"We'll deal with him."

"How?"

"The same way we dealt with you initially."

"I keep telling you guys, Ian is so much more powerful than I am."

"Yes, well, we've expanded our arsenal since we captured you."

"You think that'll be enough?"

He stares at me, again pressing his lips into a stressed line. "Let us hope so."

I let out a nervous bubble of laughter. "Great. How comforting. Let me guess. You guys haven't tested the new guns."

He cocks his head at me. "No one to test them on except you. And we'd rather not do that."

I roll my eyes. "Great."

He glances at his watch again. "Let's go."

I grab my bag and follow him down the hall toward the garage. The white vans are all lined up. Sefu approaches the second one, and a hazmat goon hands him what looks like a bulletproof vest. I can't help snorting a bit.

Sefu looks back at me.

"Ian's not going to shoot you."

He frowns at me as he accepts a helmet from the goon.

I roll my eyes. I notice all the goons have helmets with headsets, and they're all wearing body armor over their hazmat suits. No one offers me any body armor. Not that it would do any good, I guess.

Sefu does a sound check on his headset and then turns to me. "Get in. We're going."

I get in the back of the van as I've done several times before, but I can feel the nervous energy of the guys. I realize I didn't see Peter in the garage. "Where's Peter?" I ask as Sefu takes a seat next to me.

"Coming."

A goon that moves like Ocean gets in with us. He's got one of the big guns with him. The gun has truly outlandish proportions. It looks like it was cobbled together in somebody's basement for cosplay at an anime convention.

The driver says, "Moving out."

I'm pretty sure it's Goldy. I wonder where Axe is. Bay Rum is supposed to be with Peter, wherever he is.

"Is someone guarding Jerry?" I ask Sefu.

He nods. "They're leading this little caravan in the ambulance."

The van moves forward. Not for the first time, I'm irritated that the van doesn't have windows in the back. I lean forward and watch our exit from the garage. My skin feels tingly with anxiety. I don't know where we're going, but I just want to get there without encountering Ian.

The hospital is lit up like always as we leave the garage, but the streets are nearly empty this time of night. We stop at an intersection, and I lean forward, trying to see more.

"What's wrong?" Sefu asks.

"I can't see or smell anything."

He nods. "Crack the windows," he tells the driver.

The minute the window starts to open, I know we're in trouble. I can smell Ian, and he smells like he's in a very foul mood. "Oh shit."

"What?" Sefu asks, his eyes opening in surprise.

"Let's get out of here. Drive faster. Blow through red lights, whatever—just go."

He relays what I said through the headset, and I feel the van accelerate. I want to get out and run alongside it. I hate being in this stupid box, unable to see where Ian is. A violent crash happens in front of us as a dump truck falls out of the sky into the middle of the road. It clips the van in front of us, causing it to careen out of control. Goldy hits the brakes and turns the wheel, trying to avoid the spinning van. It plows into the front window of a café while we slide into the side of the dump truck and jerk around, crunching the side of the van and throwing Ocean into Sefu.

The others seemed stunned, but I'm okay—scared to death but otherwise okay.

A thunderous voice rolls over the street. "Cupcake!"

Oh, hell no! Something snaps inside of me. That bastard might kill me, but I'll be damned if I die being called Cupcake. I kick the back doors of the van open, which isn't too hard, since they're bent inward and off track.

"It's Alma, asshole!" I shout as I get out of the van and let loose all semblance of humanity.

Chapter 35: All Hell Breaks Loose

So, there I am, a big pink demon standing in an empty street. I expected Ian when I got out of the van, but he's nowhere to be seen. I look behind me at the two vans and consider checking to see if everyone's okay.

"Cupcake, Cupcake, Cupcake," Ian says.

I whirl around, and he's strolling down the sidewalk toward me, looking like he did when we were dating, when I thought he was a sweet guy, not a soul-sucking demon.

"You've made some very bad choices, girl, but it's not too late to fix that."

I look down at my big pink belly. "The only bad choice I made was dating you, asshole."

He shakes his head at me. "Such language. You used to be so sweet."

"Well, things change." I can hear movement in the van behind me.

"This doesn't have to get ugly, Cupcake. We can end this right here, right now, with none of your little friends getting hurt."

"I don't think so."

"Fine!"

He moves faster than I would have thought possible, and suddenly, this normal-looking guy rips a power pole out of the ground like it's a toothpick. Sparks fly, and the street is plunged into darkness as he transforms into his demon self. Twice the size of the pole now, he tosses it like a javelin. Despite the sudden darkness, Ian and I can see each other just fine. He flashes his teeth and puts his head down, horns forward. Maybe this was a bad idea.

I run. But I don't have any good options. I'm hemmed in by the dump truck and the vans in the street and buildings on either side. I start to climb a four-story building with a boarded-up dry cleaner on the ground floor. I don't get very far before I feel Ian's claws digging into my shoulder.

"Not that way," he growls.

I elbow him in the face. "I'm not going with you!"
He grunts when I hit him, and his grip loosens. "Yes, you are!"

I scramble higher, my claws sinking into the plaster siding, but he grips my ankle and pulls me back down and slams me onto the street like a rag doll. I didn't grow up fighting. Three hours with a Krav Maga trainer is the sum total of my fighting experience, and that tiny woman was nothing like the huge demon who has hold of me. Still, I do my best and kick him with my other leg.

He roars at me and shows his teeth again. "Stop that!" He grips my ankle harder, his nails digging in.

He starts to drag me down the street. I claw at the asphalt, trying to find a pothole or something to gain purchase to slow him down. I grab hold of a car as we pass it, halting Ian's forward momentum. He turns around and roars at me again, showing all his sharp, scary teeth, all black and pointy, but he doesn't do anything, not really. Is he all bark and no bite? Or is he dragging me off to kill me somewhere else? I don't want to find out.

"Let go!" he growls.

I don't let go. Instead, holding onto the axle, I rip off one of the wheels and throw it at his head. He swipes at it with his free hand, knocking it aside, then punches me in the groin, or where my groin would be if this body had sexual characteristics. It hurts. It really hurts, but not like it's going to kill me, so I kick him in the gut with my free leg. His nostrils flare with rage. He flings me against a small office building on the other side of the street. I hit the brick front so hard I dent the wall like a cartoon character and bounce off back into the street. Broken glass rains down on me. He's coming for me but not in a hurry. He knows I can't get away. But then I hear it—the high-pitched whine of one of the big guns. He doesn't seem to notice, even though he has to be able to hear it too. He's too fixated on me for it to register. I force myself not to look toward the vans as I hear a second high-pitched whine. I don't want to telegraph what they're doing and give Ian time to escape. I warned him last time, and that was a mistake.

"Maybe we can work something out," I say weakly, still lying on the ground.

"Definitely," he growls and grabs my arm. "Make like a human, bitch, or I'll drag you all the way back to DC like this."

Ian jerks me to my feet just as a brilliant blue light shoots down the alley like a horizontal bolt of lightning. The shot goes between us, hitting Ian's arm and grazing mine. Ian screams, and so do I—it burns in a way I don't remember feeling when they shot me before.

"Try not to hit Alma!" I hear Sefu shout.

Ian must have heard it, too, because he turns his head to look. I take that opportunity to kick him in the knee. Thanks, Krav Maga. Unfortunately, kicking Ian's knee has no discernable effect. He punches me in the face, knocking me on my ass, then runs back across the street. He's clearly decided not to mess with these guns. I don't blame him. My arm feels like it's on fire.

I hear squealing tires and look down the street away from the vans. A vehicle I haven't seen before is barreling toward us. It looks like one of those military Humvee things, and it has a huge, weird-looking gun mounted on its roof.

Ian starts to scale the front of a building, trying to exit the street to safety. Another lightning bolt arcs from the second smaller gun and hits Ian's leg. He screams, and it slows him down, but it doesn't stop his climb toward the roof. Just as he starts over the top of the wall, a blinding white beam blasts through the night, lighting up the street like it's the middle of the day. The blast hits Ian squarely in the back, and he lets out a deep, guttural howl that rips through me.

When the flash fades, I still see an afterimage of the arc as it takes a moment for my vision to clear. The street falls into silence, but then in the distance, I hear sirens. I wonder how Sefu plans to explain all this to the cops.

To make it easier, I revert to my human form. I mold myself into a simple dress—more of a sack, really, but I'm not naked, and it's not a difficult shape to hold. Sefu walks over.

"Are you all right?"

"I think so. My arm is killing me, but I'm okay. Where's Ian?"

Peter walks up behind Sefu. "That's a good question. We need to get on top of that roof to see if there's any residue."

"Residue?" I ask. "Did you disintegrate him?"

"Good question," Peter says.

He seems almost chipper. Freak.

Two of the goons pull a ladder off the side of one of the vans and set it against the building Ian climbed. The sirens are growing closer.

Bay Rum walks up. "No sign of the creature on any of the equipment."

"Good," Sefu says. "Get the guys who were in the van with us to get out of their hazmat suits and then go deal with the police."

"Yes, sir," Bay Rum says and starts for the vans.

"Oh," Sefu says, "and get someone to tow the van out of the café."

Bay Rum turns back to look at him. "Already on their way."

"Excellent," Sefu says. "Good work." He looks at Peter. "Really good work."

"Come on," Peter says, bouncing on the balls of his feet. "Let's get up there."

I follow Peter and Sefu up the ladder. As I'm climbing, I hear one of the goons say, "What are we supposed to do with the baby? Why is he even up here?"

Baby? What baby?

Sefu asks the same thing I'm thinking.

"I don't understand," Peter says.

As I step off the ladder onto the roof, everyone is looking around except Peter. He's staring straight at me. They're all standing in a circle around a baby that's lying naked on the tar and gravel roof. I have a terrible thought that the infant must have been in one of the cars that got thrown. Poor little thing. I assume a baby couldn't live through something like that, but then there's a plaintive cry.

All the men look back at the baby like they've never seen one before.

"Oh, for goodness' sake," I say, reaching down to pick up the little guy.

"Wait!" Sefu says. "He could be injured."

I look at the baby, who is clenching and unclenching his tiny fists, waving his arms and legs, and crying. "He's not injured. He's just cold and probably hungry." I pick him up. He settles immediately, but he smells a lot like Jerry. "Guys? I think we have a problem."

Chapter 36: Some Answers

The access door opens, and Axe steps onto the roof. "Come on," he says. "There's another way out."

We follow him through the door and down five flights of stairs to another door that opens onto the street. Yet another white van is there waiting, and we all climb into the back with Axe. A goon who smells like oranges and lemons is driving. I shall call him Citrus.

The baby, who I'm fairly certain is Ian, has the dress that is not really a dress but part of me gripped in his tiny hand. It's a weird sensation.

I look at Sefu. "Listen, this baby smells like Jerry."

He holds up a hand to stop me. "We'll talk when we get back to base."

I look down at the baby. He seems so innocent and sweet, but I'm pretty sure he's Ian, although I don't understand how that's possible. I wonder if the state of the baby is permanent or if Ian will revert to form in a minute and blow apart this van and kill everyone in it, except maybe me. The thought is disquieting. I'm dreading the long drive to the second site, so I'm surprised when the van pulls into a parking garage.

"Wait, where are we?" I ask.

"Back at the hospital," Sefu says. "With this situation resolved, I thought it prudent."

"What about Jerry?"

"I've routed him back as well. With things under control, he'll be better served by staying here."

I think Sefu is making a pretty big assumption that the situation is under control, but I hold my tongue for the moment. Citrus parks the van, and we all climb out.

Sefu turns to Axe and says, "Contact the others at the site and make sure they don't need assistance."

"Yes, sir."

"Alma, come with us," Sefu says.

I follow him and Peter to Peter's lab.

Once inside, Sefu turns to me. "All right."

I blow out a frustrated breath. I'm exhausted, hungry, and confused. "'All right' what?"

Sefu frowns at me. "You said the baby smells like Jerry."

"Yes."

"I don't understand," Sefu says.

"Are you saying this is Jerry's baby?" Peter asks.

I can't help the snort that escapes. "What? That's ridiculous."

"Then what are you saying?" Sefu asks, clearly irritated.

"I'm saying I think this baby used to be a demon, but now he's human. I'm saying I think this is Ian."

Peter shakes his head. "Even if that's true, he shouldn't be a baby."

"What are you talking about?" I ask, but Peter turns to Sefu.

"If we knocked the creature back to its own dimension, it shouldn't change the state of the human host."

"Wait, what?" I say. What the hell is he talking about?

Sefu strokes his goatee. "Perhaps Ian was turned when he was a baby."

"No," I say. "Adults only. Succubi and incubi don't go after children."

Sefu cocks his head, considering. "What makes you say that? Have you ever tried to take a child's soul?"

"Of course not!"

"Then you don't know if you can or not. For that matter, have you ever tried to take a woman's soul? What about animals?"

"I was told I could only take men's souls."

"Who told you that?"

"Ian."

"Ian also told you that you had to have sex with the men to take their souls."

"Yes."

Sefu raises his eyebrows. "So we know Ian is not a good source of information. Either he intentionally lied to you, or he simply repeated things he was told but never bothered to verify."

"I'm not taking a child's soul for your—"

He holds up a palm. "No one is asking you to. I'm simply saying that you don't always have accurate information."

He has a point. "Fine. Speaking of souls, I'm hungry. Is there anyone dying upstairs?"

Sefu sighs. "Probably. Go change, and I'll find something."

I hand Ian to Sefu, but he hands him to Peter.

"Run blood work and a urine panel, and make sure he's human."

"You might want to wrap him in a blanket until we can get him some clothes," I say.

"Right," Peter says, holding Ian like he's never seen a baby before.

I walk out with Sefu. "You know he's going to need food and clothes and diapers and toys and..."

"Yes, yes," Sefu says. "But let's make sure he's human before we start setting up a nursery."

"Okay, but I wouldn't wait for the diapers if I were you."

He nods. "You seem like quite the expert."

I stare at him. "You don't have to be an expert to know that babies poop."

Bay Rum comes down the hall toward us. "Everyone is back, and they're stripping the vans so we can take them for repairs."

"Excellent," Sefu says. "I'm going to make a call, and then I'll need you to send someone up to the nursery for some essentials."

Bay Rum shifts uncomfortably. "Okay, but we can't just keep a baby. We need to—"

"That baby may not be what he seems to be. Before any other steps are taken, we have to verify that he's entirely human and will remain so."

Bay Rum nods. "Yes, sir."

"Very well. Alma, go get changed and then help Peter. I need to make a few calls, and I'll meet you back at the lab."

"Okay." I'm exhausted, and my arm still hurts, but I do as he asks.

Once in my room, I realize all my clothes are in a bag somewhere with the rest of my stuff. Great. I head back to the lab. When I reach it, I press the doorbell, and the door slides open immediately. Ian is screaming when I walk in, and Peter looks at me.

"Oh, thank God you're back. He won't stop screaming."

Ian is still naked and lying on one of the long counters between a computer and another piece of equipment. There's a little bandage on his heel.

"Didn't I tell you to wrap him in a blanket?"

Peter looks around the lab and shrugs. "What blanket?"

"Give me your jacket."

"Why?"

I roll my eyes. "Seriously? I'm going to wrap him up in it."

"Don't you have a shirt or something in your room?"

"Actually, no. I don't have any clothes, because I packed them all and haven't gotten them back. So give me your jacket."

Reluctantly, he takes off his black suit coat and hands it to me. I collect Ian from the counter and wrap him up as best I can. He calms down and snuggles against me.

"See? He was just cold." I sit down in one of the lab chairs and blow out an exhausted breath.

Peter looks at me. "You look a bit blurry around the edges."

"Yeah? Well, I'm exhausted and hungry. And I have about a million questions."

Peter opens a drawer, pulls out a granola bar, and hands it to me. It's not what I really need, but it's better than nothing. Munching on my snack, I try not to think about how incredibly weird it is to be sitting with baby Ian in my lap. But I'm not going to lie—it's hard to think about anything else.

"What did you mean when you said you knocked the demon back to its own dimension?"

Peter winces and scratches his cheek like he's unsure whether he should say anything. Sefu walks in, and Peter turns to him without answering me.

"The situation is locked down," Sefu says.

"Let me guess," Peter says. "Blown gas main."

"Yes," Sefu says. "Exploding gas covers a multitude of sins." He looks at me. "Why aren't you dressed? They're ready for you upstairs."

"I don't have any clothes. All my stuff is still in the van."

He frowns. He picks up a wall phone and presses in a code. "Bring Alma's bag from the van to the lab." He turns to Peter. "What's the verdict?"

"Like Jerry, he seems completely human. I didn't have any trouble drawing blood, and it looks completely normal under the microscope. I'm running a full panel now, but that will take a while. I still need to do an X-ray and get some other samples, but for now, he's a regular baby."

"So it worked," Sefu says.

"What worked?" I ask.

Peter and Sefu exchange a look.

"Come on!" I can't believe they're still withholding information after everything that happened today.

Sefu gives Peter a slight nod.

Peter turns to me and takes a deep breath. "The weapon was designed to force whatever was inside Ian back to its own dimension."

"Okay," I say slowly, trying to digest that. "So you're saying that some creature from another dimension is inside me too."

"Yes," Peter says.

I suddenly see a way out of my situation. "So you can shoot it out of me?"

Peter winces. "No."

I look at both of them. "Why not?"

"The gun was a prototype. It worked, obviously, but it wasn't really ready. It burned out."

"So build another one."

"We will," Sefu says. "But it's a complex build, and some of the components are difficult to acquire. You must be patient, Alma."

I stand up. "Patient? You want me to be patient after you tell me some creature from another dimension is living inside me? What the fuck? I don't want to be patient. I want this thing gone! I want my life back!"

Peter steps back, and Sefu holds up his palms.

"Calm down, Alma. We will fix it. I'm just saying it will take some time."

I realize I'm looking down at him. I take a deep breath and resume my human form. Good thing, too, because Axe walks in with my duffel bag in one hand and a plastic hospital bag in the other.

"I got what you need for the baby, boss." He hands Sefu the plastic bag and me the duffel. "Here's your stuff."

"Thanks," I say, trying to stay calm.

"Get dressed, Alma," Sefu says. "Axe will take you upstairs. You'll feel better after."

Sighing, I hand him Ian and go into the lab bathroom to change. I put on the familiar janitorial clothes and try not to get too excited about the prospect of eventually being human again. I'm so sick of this demon gig. I just want to be me.

Chapter 37: Not the Nanny from Hell

A cleaning cart is stationed by the elevator, and Axe rides up with me to the lobby. He hands me a slip of paper with two room numbers on it.

I stare at him. "Two?"

He shrugs.

The elevator door opens, and I roll the cart to the other elevators that will take me to patient rooms. On the seventh floor, I get out and roll the cart to room 701. An elderly woman lies small and frail in the bed. Damn you, Sefu. I look at the equipment hooked up to her. Low pulse oxygen, low heart rate. The whiteboard next to the bed has *DNR* written in red letters. Do Not Resuscitate. She's barely breathing and fading fast. Despite my misgivings, I'm curious as to whether this will work. I lean over and gently kiss her papery lips. Her soul slips into my mouth with no resistance. Huh. There's another lie Ian told me.

I dutifully empty the wastebasket into my cart and roll it out to the hallway. I see nurses heading toward the old woman's room, but no one is running. When I reach room 719, an elderly gentleman awaits me. I take his soul and return to the hallway. I'm torn with conflicting emotions. I'm sad for those two people, but I feel so much better. Their souls are rich and full, and I feel whole with them rolling around in my belly. I sigh. I'm so sick of this, but maybe Peter can fix me.

Axe is waiting when I return to the lobby. We ride the elevator down in exhausted silence. Axe usually radiates energy, but today, like me, he's just beat.

When we finally reach the basement, I'm not sure where I'm supposed to go, but I'm so tired I decide to go back to my room and try to get some sleep. When I open the door, I'm surprised to find Sefu sitting on the edge of the bed, holding Ian. At least they've put Ian in a proper onesie and wrapped him in a blanket with tiny elephants all over it.

"He won't eat," Sefu says.

I think about all the times Ian took hard-earned souls from me.

"Perhaps you could try," he says, holding the baby out to me.

Annoyed, I take him. "Look, the grown-up version of this kid lied to me, took my soul, bullied me, and, oh, a few hours ago, beat the crap out of me. So if you're expecting me to play nanny to this kid, think again."

Sefu sighs and holds out a bottle. "I know. But please, just until we can verify that his humanity will hold and then make other arrangements."

"How long is that supposed to take?"

"A few days, perhaps a week."

I grit my teeth. "Fine."

I look around the room. There's nowhere to sit, so I settle onto the bed with Ian and offer him the bottle. He takes it right away. Asshole.

Sefu stands. "You have the magic touch."

"Yeah, whatever. If Peter shoots me with the new gun, will I get turned into a baby too?"

Sefu blows out a slow breath. "We don't know."

I frown at him. I don't want to be a baby again. Reliving middle school? What a nightmare.

"Honestly. This is a whole new branch of science. We're mostly testing theories. We're still gathering preliminary data, Alma. I don't have answers."

"I don't understand how demons from another dimension can just take over someone's body."

Sefu sits back down on the edge of the bed. "We don't completely understand the process, either, but it's inaccurate to call them demons. They're from another dimension, which is likely completely different from ours. Perhaps the shape you take is simply what they look like."

"Okay, then why are they doing this?"

He sighs. "Again, we're not certain, but it seems to have something to do with energy exchange—although the bioenergy released from a dying human is so minuscule that we can't understand how it's of much use."

"Like, how much power?"

"Ten to one hundred millivolts. It's nothing." He shakes his head. "If these creatures really want a powerful bioelectrical punch, why aren't they going after electric eels? One eel can generate six hundred volts. That's real power."

I consider that and how souls feel different inside me, how some souls are fuller. "Maybe you're not measuring them right."

He lifts an eyebrow. "What do you mean?"

I explain about the variations in souls.

Sefu strokes his goatee and considers what I've told him. "That's intriguing. I'll discuss it with Peter. He'll likely have a great many questions."

I roll my eyes. "Of course." Sometimes, I should just keep my mouth shut.

"Although it stands to reason that the souls you find paltry are on the ten-millivolt end and the ones that seem rich are closer to one hundred."

Ian gurgles, and I put him on my shoulder to burp him.

Sefu stands again.

"Where are you going?"

"Home. I need dinner and some sleep."

I hold out Ian.

Sefu seems surprised. "What—"

"He's fed."

"Can't he just stay here with you until—"

"No. I've spent all the nights with Ian that I'm going to. You take him." I'm a little surprised when he does.

"All right, Alma. I'll see you in the morning. Get some rest."

"Good night." Despite myself, I can't help wondering where Ian will spend the night. Making me care about the baby version of him feels like his last laugh. Bastard.

I turn off the light and expect to fall asleep immediately. I'm so tired, and my belly is full. I let my human façade fall and lie back. I close my eyes, but now that I'm free from distractions, the pain in my arm is more obvious. It feels badly sunburned and also tingles like it's fallen asleep. I shift around, trying to get comfortable. I toss and turn for a while before I give up and turn on the light to look at my arm. Even though the rest of me is in demon form, my arm can't seem to stick to that. It's not as pink, and it feels like it wants to be human shaped. It's not actually going back and forth, but it feels like it wants to. Frustrated, I get out of bed and pace, trying to decide whether to see if Peter is still around and can do anything to help.

I look at the door. It's usually locked when I'm in here, but I didn't hear anyone lock it after Sefu left with baby Ian. I reach for the handle and am surprised when it turns easily. I revert back to human form and get dressed.

The halls are quiet as I walk to the lab, but there are hazmat goons at all the hallway intersections. They trust me more but maybe not that much, or maybe everyone was just so tired tonight that they forgot to lock me in. No one questions my progress toward the lab, so I continue.

I can't tell if there's a light on in the lab, and all the air scrubbers prevent me from smelling whether Peter is in there. I knock on the lab door.

Peter opens it a moment later. He's in jeans and a sweatshirt instead of his usual garb. "Alma? What are you doing up? I thought you were exhausted."

"I am, but my arm is killing me, and I was wondering if you could do anything about it."

He looks at me blankly. "Like what?"

"I don't know. I don't even know what's wrong with it. Didn't you build the gun?"

"Yes, but—well, what's it doing?"

I explain how my arm feels.

He cocks his head at me. "Hmm. Did you have any of these effects the first time we shot you?"

"No."

"Hmm."

I wish he'd stop *hmm*ing at me.

"That suggests it might be a cumulative effect. We'll have to see how long it lasts."

"Can't you give me something?"

"I suppose I could give you a pain reliever, but I can't imagine it would do you any good."

"Well, let's give it a try," I say, irritated at how indifferent he is. I'm glad he never had a flock. I don't think he's a very good priest.

He rummages around in a drawer and comes up with a generic bottle of acetaminophen. I take three.

"Do you want a glass of water?" he asks.

"No." I toss the pills in my mouth, and they just seem to fall into me. I don't even have to swallow.

"Go back to bed, then. You must be tired."

"Aren't you tired?"

"Are you kidding? I'm too excited to be tired. I got more data today than I've gotten since we started this project, and I've only scratched the surface analyzing it. I'm processing sensor data now, and I've got footage to watch from several cameras. There's loads to do. Not to mention all the tests I need to run on our little friend."

"Speaking of him, where is Ian? Did Sefu take him?"

"What?" Peter says, already distracted by something on his computer screen. "No, don't be ridiculous. The baby can't leave the facility until we're absolutely certain he won't revert to his previous form."

I hate that I care. I don't want to care, but he's a baby, tiny and vulnerable. "So where is he?"

"In the containment field."

"You left him in one of those plastic cages?"

"Yes, but—plastic?"

"Whatever they're made of. Do you have a monitor on him?"

He turns one of the screens toward me, and an image of Ian appears. He's kicking and waving his arms around and clearly screaming.

"Sound?"

Peter frowns but presses a button on the keyboard, and the room is filled with Ian's cries.

"You're an asshole."

"I can't babysit him. I'm very busy."

"Then get one of the goons to do it."

"It's not safe. He could revert."

"Dammit! You guys suck! Come on, I'll take him." I storm out the door with Peter sheepishly following me.

I stop suddenly and turn around. Peter almost runs into me, stopping short and leaving us only a couple of inches apart.

"Answer me this—is he still in there?"

Stepping back, Peter says, "I'm not sure what you mean."

"Ian. Is he in that baby?"

"The demon appears to be gone."

"I'm not talking about that. I'm talking about his memories. Jerry remembers being a demon. Does that baby remember being a demon?"

Peter raises his eyebrows. "That's an excellent question."

"What's the excellent answer?"

"I have no idea, and I'm not sure how we'd find out until he's old enough to talk."

"Are you serious?"

He shrugs. "What did you expect me to say? There's so much we don't know."

"Great."

We walk down to the containment cells. Peter opens the one he stashed Ian in, and I pick up the little guy. He stops crying. I hold him up and look him in the eye, or at least I try to. He can't seem to focus back.

"How old do you think he is?"

"Six weeks is our best guess."

He's so little and fragile. I'm guessing he weighs only about ten pounds. If Ian is in there, I can't see him.

"Fine. I'll take him back to my room. We can figure the rest out in the morning."

Peter doesn't say anything as I leave with Ian. I'm irritated as I walk through the long white hallways back to my room, but as I walk, I realize I might've made a mistake—and not just because this baby used to be Ian. I don't know what I'm going to do with him. He can't sleep with me, because I'm a big pink demon, and there's no room in the bed. Not to mention that I could roll over and crush him. I stop walking and hold the little guy out in front of me. It's weird to think of him as Ian.

"Well, little whoever you are, I can't let Peter put you back in that box."

I keep walking to my room, puzzling over what to do. When I get there, I stuff all the clothes from the dresser into one drawer, take the empty one out, and set it on the floor next to the bed. I take the blanket off my bed and make a nest of it in the empty drawer. I put the baby on top of the blanket and tuck the blanket he's wrapped in tighter around him. I guess he'll cry when he's hungry again. I assume Peter has formula in the lab, so I'll cross that bridge when I come to it.

There's a knock on the door.

I open it, and one of the hazmat goons hands me the plastic bag Axe brought down from the hospital. "Father Peter said you'd need this."

I take the bag. "Thanks."

He closes the door, but I don't hear it lock. Curious. I look in the bag and find premixed formula, a baby bottle, a bib, and a bag of diapers.

"Okay," I say to Ian. "I guess we're set for the night."

I settle on the bed and drop my good arm down so he can feel I'm there. My other arm still hurts, but I'm so tired I have to close my eyes. Hopefully, Sefu and Peter will have more answers and a solution to the baby problem in the morning.

Chapter 38: New Beginnings?

The phone rings at eight o'clock the next morning, waking me and startling Ian— who begins to scream. I pick him up and hold him close, bouncing him lightly in the crook of my arm while I reach for the phone. It's Sefu.

"Jerry is awake and asking for you upstairs."

"Okay. Come get the baby, and I'll go see him."

There is a brief pause. "Actually, take the baby with you. It might hearten Jerry to see him."

"Really? Because the previous version of this baby is why Jerry's in the hospital in the first place."

"True, but he's hardly dangerous now."

"What happened to 'he could revert at any moment'?" I'm irritated that they used that line on me to get me to take him when, clearly, they aren't really worried about it.

"That possibility seems less and less likely. All of the tests Peter ran last night came back indicating that the baby is entirely human. I think it's safe to have him around Jerry. He's in room 405."

I look down at Ian, who has calmed down and is mouthing my arm—my big, pink demon arm. It doesn't seem to bother him that I'm not human shaped, which makes me wonder how much he remembers about demons. Maybe babies just don't care. Who knows?

"Fine. Let me feed Ian and get him changed, and then I'll take him to see Jerry."

"Very good. Come to my office after."

"Yeah, okay." I hang up and set Ian in the middle of the bed while I warm up a bottle for him in the bathroom sink.

When he's fed and wearing a fresh diaper, I put him back in his same old onesie because no one thought to get more than one—like they think that's what the name means. I turn into Alma and put on jeans and a T-shirt to go upstairs.

The door opens, so since I'm apparently free to roam about, I walk down to the elevators. A hazmat-suited guard nods at me as I walk by. While I take the elevator up to the lobby, I can't help wondering how far my newfound freedom extends. I look out the glass front of the building. It's a beautiful day. *Hmm*.

I go up to Jerry's room on the fourth floor. The door is open, so I stick my head in. "Hey, Jerry! You up for visitors?"

"Absolutely."

He's sitting up and finishing his breakfast. He has fresh bandages on his arms and legs and in general looks a lot better than the last time I saw him. He smiles at the sight of Ian.

"Who's that little guy?"

I close the door. "Well, that's kind of a long story." I sit down in the chair next to his bed and proceed to tell him all of what transpired the previous day.

When I'm done, I feel wrung out.

"Daaaaaaaamn," Jerry says. He looks at Ian in my lap. "Does he know he used to be a huge demon that ran the mid-Atlantic region?"

I shrug. "No way to tell. I guess we'll ask him when he can talk."

"That's fucked up."

"Right?"

"What are they going to do with him? I mean, they can't exactly put him up for adoption. What if he remembers who he used to be? That's not something a regular person could deal with."

"I wouldn't think so, no. I mean, parenthood has its difficulties, but finding out your son used to be a giant demon isn't generally one of them."

We both laugh.

"He's a cute little guy, though," Jerry says.

I hold up Ian and touch my nose to his. "Yeah, he's pretty cute. You want to hold him?"

"I wish I could." He gestures at his breakfast tray. "But I can barely lift my fork."

I get up and sit on the edge of the bed with Ian so Jerry can hold out a finger for Ian to grasp.

"It doesn't seem possible," Jerry says.

"I know."

"Why is he a baby?"

I shrug. "They don't know if it's a side effect of the gun or if he was a baby when he was turned into a demon."

Jerry frowns. "Kids are off-limits."

"That's what I was told, too, but I was thinking about this last night when I was feeding him. You said Ian was really old. What if he was one of the first? Maybe those other-dimensional people started with babies. That kind of makes sense, right?"

"Does it?"

"Sure. Babies can't fight back, and they're malleable in ways adults aren't."

Jerry shakes his head. "Then why not just continue turning babies?"

"I don't know. It's just a thought. It may turn out to be a side effect of the gun." I realize there's something he mentioned that bothered me. "So, now that Ian isn't in charge of the mid-Atlantic region, who is?"

"I don't know. I guess Snickerdoodle, Honey Bun, or Sugar Muffin—whichever one is older or has the most incubi."

"Do you think they'll avenge Ian?"

Jerry looks nervous. "I don't know, Cup—Alma. To my knowledge, no one's ever taken out a regional head. Demons don't just go away."

"Then why isn't the whole planet overrun with demons?"

"There are more of us than you think but probably because most demons don't spawn many other demons."

"There were a lot of women in that conference room."

"Not really. Not when you consider how long Ian's been around."

"You keep saying he's really old. How old?"

"I'm not positive. He told me once he took George Washington's mother's soul, but he could've been lying. He also said he had a field day in the lost Roanoke Colony, but who knows. I know he was really old, though, because he'd spawned so many succubi."

Jerry lets out a big yawn, and I realize I've probably been here too long. There's a knock on the door, and a woman comes in to collect his breakfast tray. When she leaves, I stand.

"I should go. You look beat."

He yawns again and nods. "Come again, though, okay?"

"I will." I squeeze his fingers gently before I go.

In the elevator, I decide to test the limits of my freedom. I haven't done that in a while, so now seems as good a time as any. When the elevator doors open, I head through the lobby and out through the revolving front door into the sunshine. Not wanting to press my luck too far, I sit down on a bench near the entrance. I settle Ian on my lap and wait.

A couple of minutes later, Sefu comes out of the front entrance and joins me on the bench. "I thought we agreed you were going to come to my office when you left Jerry."

I shrug. "I thought I'd give the baby a little fresh air first." If he can use the baby as an excuse, so can I.

Sefu frowns at me.

I ignore it. "He needs more clothes."

"Yes, well, the new facility will have a nursery. The man you call Bay Rum is seeing to that today." Sefu takes Ian from me.

"You're taking him to the second site, then?"

"It's still the plan to move everyone there. We only came back here because it was convenient."

"What about me? I thought you couldn't feed me out there."

"Bay Rum actually thought of an elegant solution."

"Really?"

"He is sympathetic to your moral conundrum. Apparently, he's been thinking about it since your conversation in West Virginia."

"What's his solution?"

"End-of-life care."

"I can't just pretend to be—"

"No pretending, or at least you'd have only one persona. You'll work for an agency and actually help those who are suffering. On occasion, you will be the only one with a client, and you'll feed. It's essentially the same thing you're doing at the hospital, but better—because you'll be expected to actually do the job."

"I'm not qualified for that."

"You'll have training. In the meantime, we'll bring you back to the hospital a couple of times a week."

I don't know what to say. The idea of actually helping people who are dying before I take their souls seems slightly less problematic to me. "That sounds like I'd be leaving the facility every day to go to work. Or is one of the goons supposed to drive me around?"

"It would be a great deal of freedom for you, but I believe Bay Rum is right—you do not wish to be what you are. This is a solution to feeding you until we can figure out how to make you human again without turning you into an infant, if it was actually the gun that did that."

A van pulls up to the entrance of the hospital, and a man hops out of the passenger seat to help an elderly woman in a wheelchair out of the back. I watch as he rolls her to the door. The van pulls away, and I turn to Sefu.

"Okay. I'm in. But there's something else Jerry mentioned that I think you should know." I explain about the mid-Atlantic region and what Ian's absence might mean.

Sefu nods. "I spent most of last night thinking about what might happen now that there is a power vacuum. Jerry is wrong, though, that demons don't disappear. The world has a long history of demon hunters. We are likely the first group to turn one back into a human, but power vacuums in the demon world are nothing new."

"What happens now?"

"Likely, the same thing that happens in any organization that suddenly loses its leader—a struggle among key players to fill the void."

"Do you think they'll seek vengeance for Ian's disappearance?"

"Possibly, which is why we are moving everyone to the second site today. Go pack your things. We're leaving in an hour." He stands and walks back into the hospital, taking Ian with him.

I sit for a few more minutes on the bench, watching people come and go from the hospital. I enjoy the sunshine on my face for just a little longer before I get up and go inside. I should feel relieved: Sefu has a plan, I've got a new job, and I'll have more freedom. But I feel a strange resonance in my body, something deep and foreboding.

The elevator ride down to the basement no longer feels like a descent into prison. Instead, I feel like a rat scurrying back to the safety of its hole.

Epilogue

The Allegheny mountains are beautiful in Western Maryland. I'm not sure why that surprises me—I've just never been out here before, I guess. In my mind, Maryland is Baltimore, but apparently, there's a lot more to it. I had imagined that the second site would be another deep hole for us to scurry into, but instead, it's a broad campus surrounded by high fences, massive gates, and watchtowers. It looks like a college combined with a prison; it's pretty—until you notice those security measures.

On one of the broad lawns, I see that an aide has rolled Jerry out in a wheelchair to enjoy the sunshine. He's starting to walk in physical therapy, but at the end of a long day, he's back in the wheelchair. Ian is in his lap. Jerry's taken a real shine to the little guy, but the irony of that isn't lost on him. Ian is too young to share his thoughts, so we're all just waiting to find out what's going on inside his head. It's weird to think decades, maybe centuries, of memories are bottled up inside that baby's head. If they are, he doesn't seem distressed about it. He seems like a regular infant—if he's fed and dry and held, he's happy. But it's still weird.

Peter has yet to determine whether Ian's age shift is a side effect of the gun or if he was originally turned into a demon while he was an infant, so my status remains unchanged until we can determine whether shooting me would put me back in diapers too. What we need is another demon target, but thus far, one hasn't presented itself. I have a gnawing suspicion that will change.

Peter is very wrapped up in production of the new gun and improvements to the existing ones. I understand now why they needed a big facility like this. Peter isn't just making a prototype; he's manufacturing a small arsenal for a war we all worry might be coming. The wild card is that none of us know what a war between us and other demons is going to look like. That makes it hard to prepare.

The door to the facility opens behind me.

"Hey!" Bay Rum shouts across the lawn. "Maddy is here."

I wave at him to let him know I'm coming. I'm back to taking Krav Maga three times a week. It's not tiring, but it is useful in a fight. I haven't had one since Ian, but like everyone around here, I'm working to gain any advantage I can in future conflicts. On days I don't have Krav Maga, I'm studying to be a certified nurse's aide, taking all-day classes at the local community college. So far, one of the goons has driven me, but Sefu tells me that will change once I actually get the job. That should be soon, because it's not that long of a course, relatively speaking. I'm excited about the prospect of driving on my own, although I'm positive the car will have a tracker. I'll probably even have someone tailing me. Still, it will feel a lot like freedom, so I'll take it.

I walk back into the facility and down the long hall to the gym. I told my mother that I moved to Western Maryland for a fresh start and that the drug treatment program helped me get into community college. I don't know if drug treatment programs actually do that, but I'm pretty sure that if they did, they wouldn't funnel recovering addicts into a program that assists dying patients on serious pain meds. Did my mother question any of that? No, of course not. She's happy for me, and that's all that matters. Since I was never actually a drug addict, it's worked out okay. Of course, I'm not actually getting the training under my own name or in my own body. I'm using one of the IDs Sefu had for me: Mary Smith, dishwater blonde, five foot four, one hundred thirty pounds. It's an easy shapeshift, since she looks the most like me of all the hospital IDs.

Since I don't have access to patients yet, someone, often Sefu, drives me back to the hospital to feed. It's two or more hours, both ways, filled with mostly silence. I hate the ride so much. At the facility, I'm busy. In the hospital, I'm on task. But during the car ride, I'm left to contemplate my situation, which feels largely unchanged despite everything that's happened. I know that's not really true, but it feels true, and I hate it. I still want my life back more than anything, and the long car rides just remind me I don't have it.

Then there's the dread—the actual physical manifestation of dread that I feel whenever we leave campus. I can sense them out there, the other demons. They're watching, waiting. I'm just not sure for what. Jerry doesn't feel it. He's even lost his lingering demon funk, as has Ian. So it's just me, and I can't explain it to anyone else. But I know it's happening. And whatever's coming, it's not going to be good.

About the Author

Marie Flanigan grew up all over the Commonwealth of Virginia as the youngest of three girls. Star Wars and comic books dominated her youth. She has a couple of degrees from George Mason University and is a licensed Private Investigator. Over the years, she's been a disc jockey, a web developer, and a children's librarian.

An avid gamer, she reviews video games for GameIndustry.com. After nine car accidents, five concussions, and brain surgery, she decided that perhaps she was more suited to a quieter life. She and her husband and three dogs live happily and somewhat chaotically outside of Washington DC.

Read more at https://mflanigan.com/.

About the Publisher

Dear Reader,

We hope you enjoyed this book. Please consider leaving a review on your favorite book site.

Visit https://RedAdeptPublishing.com to see our entire catalogue.

Check out our app for short stories, articles, and interviews. You'll also be notified of future releases and special sales.